'You need me

Charlotte's eyes w

'Why don't we call a truce?' Rohan asked softly.

'That would be impossible. You hate me as much as I hate you. It's a clash of personalities; it always has been.'

'A clash of personalities?' Rohan repeated the words thoughtfully. 'I don't think that's our problem, Charlotte.'

Her fine brows slid upwards. 'Then you tell me what is.'

'Fatal attraction.'

Dear Reader

Summer might be drawing to an end—but don't despair! This month's selection of exciting love stories is guaranteed to bring back a little sunshine! Why not let yourself be transported to the beauty of a Caribbean paradise—or perhaps you'd prefer the exotic mystery of Egypt? All in the company of a charming and devastatingly handsome hero, naturally! Of course, you don't have to go abroad to find true romance—and when you're a Mills & Boon reader you don't even need to step outside your front door! Just relax with this book, and you'll see what we mean...

The Editor

Born in the industrial heart of England, **Margaret Mayo** now lives with her husband in a pretty Staffordshire canal-side village. Once a secretary, she turned her hand to writing her books both at home and in exotic locations, combining her hobby of photography with her research.

Recent titles by the same author:

BITTER MEMORIES

WILD INJUSTICE

BY
MARGARET MAYO

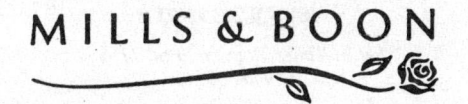

MILLS & BOON

MILLS & BOON LIMITED
ETON HOUSE, 18-24 PARADISE ROAD
RICHMOND, SURREY TW9 1SR

DID YOU PURCHASE THIS BOOK WITHOUT A COVER?

If you did, you should be aware it is **stolen property** as it was reported *unsold and destroyed* by a retailer. Neither the Author nor the publisher has received any payment for this book.

All the characters in this book have no existence outside the imagination of the Author, and have no relation whatsoever to anyone bearing the same name or names. They are not even distantly inspired by any individual known or unknown to the Author, and all the incidents are pure invention.

All Rights Reserved. The text of this publication or any part thereof may not be reproduced or transmitted in any form or by any means, electronic or mechanical, including photocopying, recording, storage in an information retrieval system, or otherwise, without the written permission of the publisher.

This book is sold subject to the condition that it shall not, by way of trade or otherwise, be lent, resold, hired out or otherwise circulated without the prior consent of the publisher in any form of binding or cover other than that in which it is published and without a similar condition including this condition being imposed on the subsequent purchaser.

MILLS & BOON and the Rose Device are trademarks of the publisher.

First published in Great Britain 1994 by Mills & Boon Limited

© Margaret Mayo 1994

*Australian copyright 1994   Philippine copyright 1994
This edition 1994*

ISBN 0 263 78621 8

*Set in Times Roman 10 on 11½ pt.
01-9409-53646 C*

Made and printed in Great Britain

CHAPTER ONE

'THIS is insanity.' Charlotte Courtenay, twenty-seven, five feet eight tall, red-haired and blue-eyed, glared hostilely at her brother-in-law. 'How can we go on working together when you make your dislike of me so clear?' And what was more a dislike she could not understand, that had manifested itself only in recent months and was disturbing in the extreme.

Pale grey eyes stared unflinchingly back. 'Don't you think I have every reason? You tricked your way into this family, pretending to love my brother when in fact the only thing you were in love with was the lifestyle he could give you.'

Charlotte gasped, but before she could say anything in her own defence Rohan went on harshly, 'Deny it if you dare. You're nothing but a scheming little gold-digger, interested only in lining your own pockets.'

'I do deny it,' she cried, unable to believe that she was hearing these things. 'How can you make such accusations? You know nothing. You see only what you want to see. I loved Glen and he loved me, and that's the sole reason I married him.'

'Are you suggesting,' he asked coldly, drawing himself up to his full height of six feet three, 'that it had nothing to do with the fact that he came from a wealthy family? That it had nothing to do with the fact that he was already rich and stood to inherit even more?'

'That is exactly what I am saying,' she riposted. They were standing in the middle of the office which had once belonged to her husband; now, since his death a few months ago, Rohan had temporarily taken over. The Lancashire textile mill had been sadly neglected during Glen's long illness, and his brother was attempting to pull it back together.

Rohan snorted savagely. 'You might have been able to pull the wool over Glen's eyes, my father's also, but don't think you can fool me so easily. I know more about you than you think, Miss Charlotte McAulay.'

Letting her breath out on a hiss of impatience, Charlotte said sharply, 'You're forgetting I'm a Courtenay now.' Goodness, all this hatred that had suddenly manifested itself; where had it come from? What was motivating him?

Grey eyes narrowed piercingly and it was as if they were looking right into her soul. 'Oh, no, I've not forgotten,' he grated. 'You took our name and you took everything else that was handed out. You cleverly duped Glen, my father also, but not me; and if it hadn't been so obvious that Glen was head over heels in love with you I would have put my foot down and stopped your marriage.'

Charlotte felt her mouth drop open as she stared at Rohan. How could he say these things? Especially after the way he had shown an interest in her himself. 'I don't know what you're talking about,' she said, blue eyes sparking, chin jutting, her whole body on the defensive. He really was the most confusing man she had ever met.

'Oh, I think you do,' he growled. 'Glen's not the first rich guy you've *professed* to have fallen in love with, is he?'

'I beg your pardon?' A frown creased her normally smooth brow. Now what was he suggesting?

Rohan's wide mouth twisted humourlessly. 'I'm talking about Barry Fernhough.'

This did shock Charlotte. 'Barry? How do you know about him?' Admittedly she had been in love with him but not because of the state of his bank balance. What a ridiculous accusation.

His eyes scorned her. 'When I heard about your *meteroic* rise to Glen's PA—a rather remarkable transition considering you had only been with the company for two years at the time, don't you think?—I thought I'd do a few investigations. I came up with some very interesting results.'

'About Barry?' She could hardly take it in that Rohan had been delving into her past. He had no right. What sort of a man was he, for heaven's sake?

'About the fact that once he experienced financial difficulties, once his business started to crumble, you wanted nothing more to do with him.'

'And that's what you think, is it?' she snapped.

'You tell me if it's any different,' he answered easily.

She could have told him that it was because Barry had been seeing another girl behind her back, but what difference would that make? He wouldn't believe her. He already had her hung, drawn and quartered, judged and found guilty. She lifted her chin. 'You're despicable.'

'I see you're not denying it.'

'Would you believe me if I did?' she flashed back.

'Not unless you had some very good excuse.'

'So what's the point?' she demanded.

'Precisely.'

'You're a bastard,' she spat.

Her thoughts flew back to when she had first met Rohan Courtenay, Glen's elder and only brother. It was at their engagement party and she had been surprised at the difference between the two brothers. Whereas Glen was fair-skinned with fine hair so pale it was almost white, Rohan had very thick dark blond hair and a much darker skin tone. They were both tall but Rohan was broader-shouldered and packed with muscle and there was really no comparison between them.

He had looked at her with eyes that were an unusual shade of grey, light in the middle with a darker ring around the iris, eyes that told her he liked what he saw. He had taken her hand in a warm, firm grip, holding it for much longer than was necessary, causing her to pull away in faint alarm.

When Rohan had asked her to dance a short time later she had wanted to refuse but knew it would be discourteous; and Glen had willingly surrendered her to his brother, pleased that the two of them had finally met.

Rohan had held her close, *too* close, his hand firm on her back, sending unexpected shivers through her veins, a whole new flood of surprising emotions. She could not believe that she was feeling such a response to a complete stranger. She loved Glen, didn't she? She was going to marry Glen. She must ignore these alien feelings, keep this unfortunately attractive man at a very long distance.

'How did you meet Glen?' His voice had been deep and gravelly, scraping along her nerves, vibrating through her body, creating totally new and alarming sensations. His aftershave had been expensive and spicy and exotic and he had overpowered her with his presence.

She had wanted to pull out of his arms but knew that Glen was watching them and so had had to pretend that nothing was wrong, that she was completely happy to be dancing with this man she had heard so much about. Glen had admired his older brother tremendously, had always regretted that he lived so far away, that he didn't come home very often.

'I became Glen's PA when he took over after your father retired,' she told him, and a gentle, unexpected courtship had followed; a pleasant, happy three years that had ended with him asking her to marry him.

'And before that?'

'I've always worked for the company, ever since leaving secretarial college.' She was glad they were talking; it helped relieve the considerable tension that had somehow built up inside her.

It was, however, a relief when the dance ended, when he took her back to Glen who was waiting for her, a happy smile on his boyishly handsome face. Although Glen was twenty-eight he did not have the maturity of Rohan at five years older and again Charlotte could not help comparing the two of them.

'Is something wrong?' asked Glen a short time later. 'You've gone very quiet.'

Charlotte smiled and shook her head. 'Of course there's nothing wrong, darling.' And she made a determined effort to enjoy herself, to forget Rohan and the unfortunate effect he was having on her. It was difficult to ignore him, though, especially when he seemed to be watching her every move. It got to the pitch when she could feel him looking at her even though her back was turned. It was an eerie feeling.

'What do you think of my brother?' It was almost midnight now and Charlotte and Glen were doing a slow dance together.

She glanced across at Rohan who had a girl in white clinging so close they were almost one, and pulled a wry face. 'He's not what I expected.' In fact a far cry; she had expected an older version of Glen; someone kind and gentle and undemanding; instead she had found an impossibly attractive man capable of turning her defences upside-down, who had triggered an instant chemical reaction that had taken her so much by surprise that her head was whirling and she wanted nothing more than to escape this party.

'But you do like him?' Glen seemed anxious that she should approve.

She smiled then, softly, warmly. Not for anything would she hurt this man she was going to marry. 'Yes, I like him.'

Glen relaxed and looked pleased and when a short while later Rohan asked her for another dance she had no choice but to accept.

Charlotte was wearing a backless black dress with narrow *diamanté* straps and Rohan's hand moved in a subtle yet insidious caress over her naked skin, sending unnerving tremors through her whole body. She had heard of love at first sight but this wasn't love, it was instant animal attraction; nothing more, nothing less; a physical response to each other that nothing could stop—except distance!

'I don't see any members of your family here,' Rohan said softly, questioningly.

'I'm an only child,' she told him, shocked to hear how husky her voice sounded.

'And your parents?'

She lifted her shoulders in a rueful gesture. 'My parents don't particularly care what happens to me.'

He frowned, dark eyebrows drawing together over his unusual grey eyes. 'You don't get on with them?'

'My father never gets on with anyone, I'm afraid,' she told him wryly. 'He's a law unto himself; and my mother—I think because she feared my father—showed me so little affection as a child that as soon as I was old enough I left home.'

'So you could say we're two of a kind?' There was a glint in his eye as he spoke, a curve to his generous lips.

Charlotte's heart went into panic and she shook her head firmly; she did not want anything that would link her to this man. 'I wouldn't say that at all.' According to Glen Rohan was headstrong and fiercely independent, an entrepreneur at any early age and now head of his own multi-national concern. 'You didn't leave home because you weren't loved, but because you wanted to make a lot of money.'

'That is true,' he agreed. 'Do your parents know about your engagement party?'

'Of course,' she answered, 'but we've grown so distant over the years that I didn't expect them to come.' Nor had she wanted them to, if the truth were known. There was always the chance that her father would embarrass her with his loud talk and tendency to argue with almost everyone he met.

The Courtenays were so different. Glen was gentle and kind and considerate and treated her with far more love and respect than she had ever been shown at home. His father, Douglas Courtenay, was a charming gentleman as well, a bit proud, and occasionally authoritarian, although Glen had said that he'd mellowed over the years. Here was the love and security that she craved, and, although she had no doubt in her mind that she loved Glen, it had helped that he came from a stable and loving background.

Glen's mother had died a few years earlier and it was from her that he had got his sunny nature; Charlotte had somehow expected Rohan to be of the same mould. How wrong she was; he clearly took after his father; he even had the same proud tilt to his head, the aquiline nose, the deep-set eyes—and the ability to make a woman feel good!

Charlotte balked at this thought but it was true. She had never felt like this in her life before, not even with

Barry whom she had previously been engaged to. What a disaster that had turned out to be; she preferred not to think about it.

Rohan had a charisma that could not be ignored, a presence that was overwhelming; he made her feel that she was the only interesting girl in the room—and the unfortunate part about it was that she was responding! He was definitely a woman's man and she pitied the poor girl he finally married; she would be frightened to take her eyes off him.

'It is a shame you don't get on with your parents,' he said. 'Have you found it very difficult living on your own? Financially, I mean. Times are very tough. You must have thought you'd landed on your feet when you got the job as Glen's personal assistant?'

Charlotte eyed him with some suspicion, sure that she detected something behind his words. 'What are you saying?'

Rohan lifted his wide shoulders and smiled disarmingly. 'Nothing at all. I've unfortunately met a lot of women in my time who marry their bosses simply to improve their lifestyle. I can see you're not like that.'

She relaxed and the music stopped and he took her back to her smiling fiancé. 'You're a lucky guy, Glen,' he said. 'I don't mind telling you that if I had met Charlotte first you wouldn't have stood a chance.'

Glen looked pleased by this compliment and he put his arm about Charlotte's waist and held her close. She turned to him and kissed his cheek and when she looked back Rohan had gone.

She saw no more of Rohan until the party ended and everyone had left the hotel ballroom hired for the occasion. A taxi had been ordered to take her back to her tiny flat in a Victorian house in Blackburn and she was saying goodbye to her future father-in-law.

Glen and Rohan stood close by, and she hoped fervently that Rohan would do or say nothing to upset her equilibrium further. Tonight had not been entirely what she'd expected and it was essential now that she escape as quickly as possible.

Glen had previously suggested that she stay the night at Frenchwood Manor, their home on the outskirts of Clayton-le-Moors, and she was glad now that she had refused, because the thought of sleeping in the same house as Rohan, perhaps even in the next bedroom, was too scary for words. Lord, she would never be able to sleep knowing he was there.

How, in the space of one evening, he had managed to confuse her to such an extent she did not know, but something had definitely happened and the more space that was kept between them the better.

When it was Rohan's turn to say goodbye he took her hand in both of his and she felt their warmth and strength, but more than that she felt a charge of electricity surge through her that was beyond comprehension, that told her how dangerous this man was to her peace of mind.

'It has been a delight meeting you,' he said, his grey eyes steadfast on hers, giving nothing at all away of the feelings that she felt sure he too was experiencing. 'Glen is indeed a lucky guy.'

When Charlotte got home it was not to sleep, it was to wonder at this man who had erupted so shockingly into her life. She had to shut him out, she had to ignore him, ignore these feelings which raged inside her. They were indecent and unwanted and entirely foreign to her nature.

But telling herself what she had to do and actually carrying it out were two different matters. He had invaded her mind and her privacy and there was no escape.

She even dreamt of him; he and Glen became one until in the end she did not know which brother was making love to her.

She woke feeling hot and uncomfortable and totally unsettled, and even more unhappy because she had been invited to dinner at the Courtenay house as Rohan was going back to his London apartment tomorrow.

To give Rohan his due he behaved with the utmost propriety, but nevertheless the attraction was still there. It amazed Charlotte that neither of the others noticed because it seemed to her that the air fairly crackled with tension and electricity, that sparks flew from her to Rohan and back again, while they each carefully maintained an expected friendly but impersonal façade.

It was the most difficult evening of her whole life. She still loved Glen; there was no doubt in her mind about that. She did not want this excitement, this sexual craving; it was lunacy; and if they gave in to it and satisfied their lust, which was all it was, she insisted to herself, it would be gone all too soon; it was a transient thing. And not only that, it would ruin her relationship with Glen.

Her love for this younger Courtenay was on a different level; it was gentle, yes, but it was complete and entirely safe. And boring, said a little voice inside her, but she chose to ignore it.

Charlotte did not see Rohan again until her wedding a few months later. She had tried, in the interim period, to push him right out of her mind. It was difficult but because of his absence she had succeeded to a certain degree.

Until they met at Glen's house the day before the wedding! It was as though he had never been away. It was still there, this surging and unbelievable attraction, this desire to be ravaged by him, to forget everything that was sane and sensible and give her body to his. It was shocking, and he felt the same way too, she was positive. They both forced themselves to keep out of each other's way.

He was Glen's best man and in his speech he repeated his statement that if he had met Charlotte first Glen wouldn't have stood a chance. He made it sound like a joke but Charlotte's cheeks burned and she refused to look at him, turning to Glen instead, smiling fondly, taking his hands and squeezing them, trying to dispel all disquieting thoughts.

They honeymooned in the Bahamas and gradually Charlotte became at peace with herself. Glen was all she had ever wanted: a gentle, considerate lover, and a good companion; there was nothing to mar her happiness. He would never set her on fire, she knew that, but she convinced herself that it was not important, that compatibility was more essential, and they certainly had that. No cross words, no disagreements, nothing except peace and tranquillity.

They returned to the house Douglas Courtenay had had built for them as a wedding-present in the grounds of Frenchwood Manor. Far enough away for them to be independent, close enough for Douglas to feel that his son had not deserted him as Rohan had.

Since his wife died he had complained increasingly of loneliness and Glen loved him too much to want to go and live in another corner of the country. Besides, he had the business to look after—and his father liked regular reports on how it was doing. Glen was content, Douglas was content, and Charlotte told herself that she was content too.

During the three years she was married to Glen Charlotte saw little of Rohan. She had the feeling that it was deliberate on his part and was grateful to him.

He came home at Christmas and on his father's birthday, but that was about all.

And now, here they were, standing in Glen's old office, facing each other like two opponents in a boxing ring. 'You had no right at all going around asking questions about me, trying to dig up dirt when none was there,' she accused him angrily.

'If I hadn't,' he told her, 'I wouldn't have found out what you were like. It was a disappointment, I agree; you were so clever, you almost had me fooled. I thought that my dear brother had found himself a wife in a million.' His eyes flashed a look of pure hatred, his lip curling contemptuously. 'I did not like being taken in.'

'If you really did think I was after an affluent lifestyle, then why didn't you say something to Glen?' she asked bitterly. 'He would soon have told you that you were barking up the wrong tree.'

Rohan looked at her as though she were out of her mind. 'You and I both know he would not have listened. Besides, I did not want to spoil his happiness. Lord knows he didn't have a very good life.'

Prone to illness, Glen had spent most of his boyhood years in and out of hospital and even as a man he had developed pneumonia twice. The years Charlotte had known him had been some of his best—until he had suddenly taken ill again. She would never, ever forget the day she was told he only had a few months to live.

Thinking about Glen now and listening to Rohan's harsh accusations made Charlotte fiercely angry. 'Yes, I made him happy,' she said, 'and I have no regrets. I did nothing of which I am ashamed. But I'm certainly not going to stay around here and be insulted. I've had enough; you can tell your father whatever you like but from now on I want nothing more to do with Courtenay Textiles.'

'Oh, no.' Rohan's nostrils flared and his eyes narrowed savagely on hers. 'You're not getting away that easily. You got this company into difficulties, you're going to help straighten it out.'

Charlotte gasped. '*I* did? How do you make that out?' He really was an amazing man, coming up with all sorts of unfounded accusations that would have been laughable had he not been so serious.

'You neglected it.'

She shook her head in open-mouthed astonishment. 'What did you expect me to do, come to work every day while my husband was ill? Maybe that's the sort of thing you would have done—making money means more to you than it does to me—but I couldn't be like that. I put Eric Shotton in charge and Douglas told me to take as much time off as I liked.'

'Shotton knew nothing,' Rohan snarled; 'he was hopeless, and if he hadn't left of his own free will I would have sacked him.'

Charlotte remembered that Eric had left the company soon after Rohan took over, declaring that he'd got another job in the south of England. How true that was she would never know, but Rohan had no right to blame her.

'Maybe I did make a mistake in thinking he was capable,' she admitted, 'but you cannot blame me entirely. Glen needed me. Lord, you're an insensitive brute.'

His eyes were hard. 'I believe you more or less ran the company, the financial side at least.'

Charlotte inclined her head. 'Yes, I did help Glen; he was never very good with figures.'

'Is that so?' he asked coldly. 'Or was it a clever, tactical move on your part? Did you think to make yourself indispensable? Was it perhaps your ambition to take over the company completely one day?' His lip curled in derision as he spoke, his eyes as cold and hard as flint. 'I believe you went on a business management course?'

Her chin lifted. 'That was Glen's idea.'

Brows rose. 'Or you very cleverly let him think it was?'

'God, you're a swine.' Charlotte lifted her hand to take a swipe at him, but he was quicker than she and caught it in a punitive grip.

'Never, ever try to hit me,' he told her through gritted teeth, 'or I might forget that I'm a gentleman and hit you back.'

Charlotte wondered where the physical attraction had gone. For three years they had studiously avoided each other, both wanting to protect Glen and keep him happy, both hiding their own electric feelings; and now Glen was gone and that was gone too. It took some understanding.

She tried to twist away from him. 'I doubt you've ever been a gentleman,' she snapped. 'You're really showing your true colours now, aren't you? I cannot believe that you've had the temerity to dig into my past like you have. You had no right; you were invading my privacy. You're a bastard and I——'

Her words were cut short as he pulled her hard against him and his mouth came down upon hers.

It was their first kiss ever and Charlotte fought with every ounce of her strength. The times she had imagined such a thing, had even dreamt of him kissing her, and now the kiss was taken in hatred and she revolted against it; she pushed at him furiously. 'You swine,' she muttered against his mouth, 'let me go.'

However, somewhere, down in the deepest recesses of her consciousness, she felt the stirring of a response, rejected immediately with the utmost horror that she could feel even the merest flicker of pleasure. This man was her enemy now, she must never, *ever* forget that; never,

ever give way to him. He had said some unpardonable things, made the most astounding accusations, and she hated him with every fibre of her being.

'What did you do that for?' she asked fiercely, when he did finally release her.

'Because it was the only way to shut you up.'

Her eyes blazed. 'Don't do it again.'

'Then don't ever rant and rave,' he answered back; 'it's not ladylike.'

She gritted her teeth and clenched her lips, glaring at him furiously. 'It's difficult to feel like a lady when you're at the receiving end of your whiplash tongue.'

'The truth hurts, does it?' he asked with an arrogant lift of his head, a sudden mocking smile curving his mouth.

'You wouldn't know the truth if it hit you in the face,' she protested. 'You just hate to think that your brother was happy with a girl you once wanted, and you hate to think that I preferred him to you. It's your ego that's hurt, nothing else, and you thought you'd see if you could dig up some dirt to try and hurt me.'

Charlotte did not know why she was saying these things—they were as wildly unjust as his accusation— but he made her angry, and his kiss had upset her even more, though she would never admit it. 'I've had enough,' she said angrily, and, turning on her heel, she headed for the door.

'I trust you're not thinking of leaving altogether?' his taut and angry voice followed.

She eyed him coldly. 'Would you stop me if I were?'

'Not physically,' he admitted. 'I prefer to conduct myself with more dignity. I am simply requesting that you stay and help me pull this company back together.'

'*Help* you?' Charlotte's eyes were sceptical. 'You appear to have taken over. All I do is carry out your orders.' It was a far cry from the days when she was Glen's PA and had her own secretary. Louise had gone long since. Now she was to all intents and purposes a junior and Rohan was intent on working her into the ground.

'Whatever you care to think,' he said, 'do I have your word?'

Charlotte lifted her shoulders. What could she say? She would do it for Douglas's sake, for Glen's sake, but not for Rohan's. She met his eyes. 'I'll stay.'

CHAPTER TWO

BACK out in her own office Charlotte sat at her desk and tried to take in all that had happened in the last few unbelievable minutes. There had most definitely been a difference in Rohan's attitude towards her since Glen's death but she had never dreamt that he was harbouring such deep and dark thoughts.

She had concluded that it was because he was upset by what had happened to his brother, that he could even be worrying because he was neglecting his own affairs, but nothing like this; certainly nothing like this. And to think that he had lived with this knowledge for over three years and never said anything. It must have festered and grown inside him and now he was taking great pleasure in throwing everything at her.

And the worst thing of all was that she still felt a tiny spark of awareness—faint and weak but there! It was madness after all he had said to her, after all the untrue accusations he had made; it should have been killed stone-dead, every last fragment of it.

It was amazing, too, how he had found out about Barry. Why had he even thought to check up on her? She remembered now their conversation when he had said something about her finding it difficult to manage on her salary, lucky that she had fallen in love with Glen; and when she'd asked him what he meant he'd made light of it. It was obvious now that he'd had these suspicions even then.

For the rest of the day Charlotte was so much on edge that she could not think straight, and when Rohan asked her the same question three times and she could not answer him sensibly she knew it was time to call it a day. She picked up her bag and her jacket and said, 'Excuse me, Rohan, I am leaving.'

He made a point of looking at his gold Cartier watch.

'I don't care what time it is,' she flung at him; 'I have a headache and I'm going.'

'Discovering that I know the truth has upset you, has it?' His sardonic smile did nothing to appease her anger.

Charlotte did not have red hair for nothing. It was slightly longer than shoulder-length and naturally wavy, and she tossed it now with a flash of her blue eyes. 'Yes, you've upset me, but not because you've hit on the truth, but because you've made assumptions that are totally incorrect.'

'You're a very good liar.' He took a step across the room towards her, smiling still, annoying her even more.

'I never lie,' she countered sharply. 'You're the one who's got your facts wrong. If you hate me why don't you let me go instead of insisting that I stay until everything's running smoothly again?'

'I don't hate you, Charlotte.' Now he was standing close—too close for comfort. 'Let's say it's your avaricious nature I'm averse to; that aside you're a very attractive young lady.' His hands closed on her arms and his head once again began to swoop towards hers.

This time Charlotte was ready for him and she wrenched herself away. 'You're despicable; keep your hands off me.' She flew over to the door and without even looking at him again yanked it open. She was very tempted to slam it behind her, but instead closed it quietly. She shouldn't let him get to her, she thought as she stood a moment trying to regain her composure. Her conscience was clear; she had no need to worry.

When the door was snatched open she gave a start of surprise. Rohan smiled, though it held little pleasure. 'I'm glad you've not gone yet. I forgot to tell you, my father has invited you up for dinner tonight. Around eight. It's his birthday, so please don't disappoint him.'

It took five minutes to reach Douglas Courtenay's house. It was now seven minutes to eight. Charlotte was ready but still she hesitated.

She was deeply annoyed with herself for forgetting her father-in-law's birthday and put it down to the fact that Rohan's presence in the office had been so unsettling that she had scarcely had time to think of other things. Usually Douglas hinted mischievously that he had a birthday coming up, but because she had seen so little of him lately—her own fault because she had stopped going to see him when Rohan came home—and because he was a shadow of his former self since Glen's death, nothing had been said.

Armed with a card now and a bottle of the older man's favourite cognac, she stood dithering, and then the thought that Rohan might easily take it into his head to come and fetch her made Charlotte jump into action.

Wearing her favourite ivory knitted dress, with a long gold chain and gold pendant earrings—both presents from her husband—and a warm ivory shawl about her shoulders, she trekked the few hundred yards along the path through the grounds of Frenchwood Manor. It was not really a manor house; it was a modern mock-Tudor building, with five bedrooms and three reception-rooms, but Douglas had called it a manor because a real Tudor manor house had once stood on the same spot.

The original had been destroyed by fire twenty years ago and the owners had been so distraught that they had sold the whole estate. Douglas had bought it for his wife because she had always loved this particular area and he had had the present house built to her specification. French was her maiden name and it was surrounded by woods—hence the name.

The front door opened as Charlotte approached the house and Rohan came out to greet her. 'I was beginning to think you weren't coming.' His tone was sharp and accusatory. 'All the other guests are here.'

Charlotte had seen the cars lining the drive, had been surprised because she thought it was a private family affair, but relieved too because it would help take some of the pressure off her. 'I said I would.' Her tone was equally caustic.

Compelled to brush past Rohan as she entered, Charlotte became aware that he was using a different aftershave. It was more musky than his normal one, more evocative, and it heightened her senses and made her remember sensations she preferred to forget. It hadn't escaped her that he looked magnificent in a white dinner-jacket and a rich purple bow-tie. She might hate the man now but she could still appreciate his exceptional good looks.

Rohan took her elbow as he led her into the crowded drawing-room and the heat from his hand felt like a branding-iron. Some of the guests were strangers, some she already knew, and she smiled politely as they made their way towards Douglas, who was seated at the far side of the room.

His face lit up when he saw his daughter-in-law. 'Charlie! When Rohan sprang this surprise party on me I hoped he had invited you as well.' He patted the seat at his side. 'Come and sit by me. We have so much to talk about.'

Charlotte discovered it was Douglas's sixtieth birthday and cursed herself anew for not remembering. Douglas did not seem to mind that she had forgotten, though, content with the fact that she was here.

At the dinner-table she was seated between Rohan and his father and could not help noting how alike they were. Both tall, autocratic men, with strong faces, well-marked brows and keen, all-seeing eyes. Glen had been nothing like either of them, and Charlotte wished she had met his mother; she would have liked to be friends with the woman whom her husband took after.

Ignoring Rohan, she concentrated her attention on her father-in-law, telling him briefly, in answer to his questions, about their efforts to pull the firm back together, making him laugh with the odd anecdote. The party was doing him good. He was visibly much more cheerful than he had been at any time during the last months.

Rohan was talking to an attractive brunette on his other side, whom Charlotte understood to be his cousin, and she was not aware that he was registering her entire conversation until he muttered fiercely, 'Still buttering up to my father, I see.'

'Is it a habit of yours, listening to other people's conversations?' she enquired sharply.

'When they concern my father, yes.' His grey eyes bored into hers, piercing in their intensity. 'And I don't think you should be discussing business; if my father wants to know anything I will tell him myself.'

'I've only answered his questions,' she snapped. 'What am I supposed to do, ignore them?'

'I know all that you've said,' Rohan growled. 'Now let that be an end to it. It is not your place to talk of such matters.'

He meant that she no longer had any position of responsibility within the company. Charlotte's blue eyes flashed. 'You're a swine.' And she turned back again to Douglas.

When the older man looked at her, his grey eyes, so like his son's, were concerned, and it was very apparent that he had been fully aware of the angry discourse going on at his side, even though he had perhaps not heard every word that they'd said. 'You don't like Rohan, do you, Charlie?' he asked, his tone sad.

It's your son who doesn't like me, she wanted to reply, but somehow managed a wintry smile. 'He's not exactly my type, I agree, and we don't always see eye to eye, but I wouldn't go so far as to say that I don't like him.'

Douglas looked disbelieving. 'But he's the reason you don't come to see me any more, isn't he?' he asked sorrowfully.

Charlotte clamped her lips and nodded.

His sadness deepened. 'Is there anything I can do to help? I hate to see you two at loggerheads.'

'I hate it too,' confessed Charlotte. 'I guess it's just a clash of personalities. There's nothing anyone can do.'

'It's a pity,' the older man murmured. 'Perhaps when he has straightened things out and found someone to take charge then I'll see more of you?'

Charlotte felt bitter that they were thinking of recruiting a new manager. It proved that neither of them thought she was capable, not even Douglas, and he must have known how much effort she had put in during the eight years she had worked for them.

However, she hid her feelings and put her hand reassuringly on Douglas's arm. 'I promise I'll come up and see you more often.' Out of the corner of her eye she saw Rohan looking at her. To hell with him, she thought; I don't care what he thinks, and she perversely leaned towards Douglas and kissed his cheek.

The older man covered her hand with his own, and there was a moment's bonding between them before they resumed eating their excellent veal escalopes.

Throughout the rest of the meal Charlotte was vividly conscious of Rohan's anger but she tried not to let it bother her, and when everyone retired to the lounge for their coffee and liqueurs Douglas insisted on keeping her at his side.

Rohan was still busy entertaining his beautiful cousin, Merelda, giving her his undivided attention, and the girl in return played up to him for all she was worth. At last Charlotte felt that she could relax, though, to her own annoyance, she constantly found her eyes drawn in his direction.

There were other girls in the room too who could not keep their eyes off Rohan, all either distant relatives or the daughters of Douglas's friends. He was certainly the most handsome and charismatic man in the room but little did any of them know what a fierce temper he had, what it was like to be flayed by his sharp tongue. She felt like getting up and shouting a warning to every one of them.

When Charlotte excused herself from Douglas's side to go to the bathroom she thought Rohan was too preoccupied with his cousin to notice, and was startled when his hand fell on her shoulder as she moved along the hallway, spinning her to face him, his grip almost paralysing.

'I think you've monopolised my father for long enough,' he growled.

Charlotte glared back into the fierceness of his eyes. 'Douglas enjoys my company; we have lots to talk about.'

'He does have other guests,' Rohan insisted.

She saw his point but had no intention of admitting it. She felt safe by Douglas's side; proved right now by the fact that Rohan had pounced on her the second she moved.

'So I suggest you circulate and let others have a chance to talk to him.'

'What are you afraid of?' she asked haughtily.

'Let's say I know the way your mind works.' His tone was hard, his eyes cold on hers. 'Keep on the old man's side, that's your motto, isn't it? Not content with what Glen left you, and the money for his not inconsiderable insurance policy, you want a share of my father's wealth as well.'

'How dare you?' Furiously Charlotte raised her hand but again, before it could make contact on Rohan's cheek, he caught her wrist in a grip so strong that she cried out in pain. 'Let me go, you swine,' she yelled, 'you're hurting me. You're a bastard and I hate you and——'

Her harsh words were cut off instantly when his mouth descended on hers. Again he took her completely by surprise, and this time it was more than a faint feeling that surfaced in the pit of her stomach. It was like liquid fire, spreading rapidly through her veins, growing out of all proportion, and in desperation she pushed and struggled and did her utmost to escape. 'You beast, let me go,' she cried when he lifted his mouth for an instant.

His laughter was mocking and loud. 'I will let you go when I'm good and ready.' And again his mouth captured hers.

No matter how much Charlotte fought she could not free herself; he was far too strong and determined. With one hand on her back, the other cupping her head, there was no escape. But the kiss could not go on forever, she told herself, especially if she did not respond! He would not like that. So she kept her lips clamped, her whole body rigid, until finally he thrust her from him, his face dark with anger.

'You're despicable, Rohan Courtenay,' she cried. 'If kissing a woman is the only way you can shut her up I feel sorry for you.' And with that she swung on her heel and ran up the stairs.

Safely behind a locked door, Charlotte took her time, not at all sure that Rohan wouldn't be waiting ready to carry on his concerted attack. It looked as though there was going to be no end to his accusations. And they all came down to the one thing—money!

It was nice, she had to admit, that she had a house and didn't have to worry where her next penny came from, but it was not of paramount importance; the man was crazy if he thought that. She was desperately saddened by Glen's death, would never be able to understand the reason he had been taken from her so young; and even if he had left her nothing it would not have mattered. Money had never entered into their relationship. She had wanted security, yes, but of a different kind: security in love, security in a good home life, security in knowing that she had a man at her side who would always treat her well.

As for Rohan claiming she wanted a share of Douglas's wealth as well, that was ridiculous. He was only sixty, for heaven's sake. Did Rohan expect her to sit around waiting for him to die also? Or did he think she had other, more devious plans lurking in the back of her mind?

She put her hand to her head, feeling a very real headache coming on. How she would love now to creep out of the house and go home.

To Charlotte's relief Rohan was nowhere in sight when she went back downstairs. She was halfway across the lounge when she was waylaid by a man she had seen eyeing her all evening. Although she knew most of the people present, if only by sight, this man was a stranger to her.

'Hello there, where has a beautiful girl like you been hiding herself all her life?' He was only an inch or so taller than herself, tow-headed, with a ruddy complexion, and unusual green eyes—and a loud voice! He was well-built and looked as though he spent most of his time out of doors.

'Excuse me?' She looked at him coolly, not welcoming this intrusion. She wanted to get back to the safety of her father-in-law's side.

'I've not seen you before,' he said easily. 'My name is Jonathan Herald, and yours is?'

Charlotte grimaced and gave in. 'Charlotte Courtenay.'

'Courtenay?' he asked with a frown. 'Then you must be——'

'Yes, that's right, Glen's widow,' she cut in sharply, more sharply than she would have otherwise spoken if it had not been for Rohan upsetting her.

'Hell, I'm sorry, I didn't know. I've been working abroad these last few years. Glen was a friend of mine at school. It's darned bad luck; you have my condolences.'

Charlotte could feel other people watching them and wished he would keep his voice down. His bluffness reminded her of her father. 'Thank you,' she said quietly.

'Lord, it's hot in here; what do you say to a walk out in the fresh air?'

He was certainly not backward in coming forward, thought Charlotte as she shook her head. 'I don't think so, but thanks for the offer anyway.'

'At least may I sit and talk to you? I've not met a single girl here tonight who hasn't eyes for anyone except your brother-in-law. Rohan has everything going for him, don't you think?'

Charlotte shrugged. 'If you prefer his type.'

Jonathan lifted thick untidy brows. 'You don't, I take it?'

'Not really,' she replied.

He looked pleased and for the next hour she could not get away from him. She was not in the least attracted to Jonathan; he was too rough and ready, not her type at all, but at least he was a welcome diversion. Rohan had been right in one thing: she could not monopolise her father-in-law all evening.

She discovered that Jonathan had been working on a ranch in Texas, had come home for three months, and was then going back again. He was entertaining in his very forthright way and although he seemed attracted to her she could not envisage herself ever dating him.

Although, perversely, when she saw Rohan's disapproval, the harsh frown on his face that spoke a thousand words, she pretended an interest in Jonathan that she did not feel, leaning provocatively towards him, touching his arm, laughing into his face. He was proving the foil that she needed.

When the first guest left Charlotte felt relief because it meant that she too could now make a move. 'I'll walk you back,' said Jonathan, joining her as she stood up.

'I'm sorry, Jonathan,' cut in Rohan, appearing miraculously by their side, 'but *I* am taking Charlotte home.' His harsh voice brooked no refusal.

Jonathan looked at Rohan and Charlotte could see him debating whether to argue, then he shrugged, obviously thinking better of it, perhaps not wanting to cause a disturbance at Douglas's party. 'I'll be in touch,' he said to Charlotte, touching her hand briefly before turning away.

'You had no right doing that,' whispered Charlotte fiercely, her whole body rigid, her eyes blazing. 'How did you know I was thinking of leaving?'

He smiled, a curious smile that made her feel uneasy. 'Body language, my dear Charlotte. I've been watching you all evening. And you're a fool even to think of letting a strange man walk you home.'

'I could see no harm in it,' she protested. 'He's a friend of the family, isn't he?'

'Hardly,' Rohan barked. 'His father is a friend, Jonathan isn't. I don't like the guy; he's not to be trusted. He's been back a couple of weeks and has already dated half a dozen different girls.'

'You're a fine one to talk,' retorted Charlotte. 'You've been surrounded by girls all evening.' The moment the words were out she regretted them; she did not want him to know that she had been watching him as well.

'The point is *I* won't be trying to talk my way into anyone's bed,' he rasped.

'You're suggesting that's what Jonathan would have done?' she asked, shocked.

'I am.'

'And do you think I'd have let him?'

'You seemed mighty friendly.'

'He was interesting to talk to; I could hardly ignore him.' She was offended that Rohan could even think such a thing. 'Excuse me, I want to say goodbye to Douglas.'

Her father-in-law was disappointed that she was leaving, and made her promise again to come up and see him more often. 'I miss you, Charlie, I really do. Don't let Rohan put you off.'

She promised, though she was not sure that she would keep her word, and then Rohan took her arm and led her outside. To her relief, once clear of the house he let her go. She was angry with herself for feeling anything other than animosity, and could not understand why these old feelings had resurfaced, especially in the face of his completely unfounded accusations.

'How much do you know about Jonathan? What has he told you about himself?' Rohan's questions were fired at her tersely.

Charlotte looked at him coldly. 'I don't see that it has anything to do with you what we were talking about.'

'You're refusing to answer my questions?' He shot her a glance but did not halt his pace; they were almost marching along the drive.

'You bet I am,' she told him. 'You're the last person I'd talk to about friendships.'

'Friendships?' he pounced. 'You're calling it a friendship after just a couple of hours? I have to say one thing about you—you're consistent.'

Charlotte frowned. 'I don't know what you're talking about.'

'The size of the man's bank balance.'

Charlotte stopped suddenly, her whole being affronted and outraged. 'Your mind's perverted,' she cried.

He halted too, turning to face her, the light from a brilliant moon capturing the harshness of his features. 'You're denying the fact that you know Jonathan Herald is a wealthy man?'

'Yes, I am,' she countered savagely.

'He didn't tell you that he works a ranch in Texas?'

'Yes, of course he told me,' she replied, her eyes bright with anger, 'but I hardly think working on a ranch would make him a rich man.'

Rohan's mouth hardened. 'He doesn't simply work *on* it, he owns it. From all accounts it's huge; he has several thousand head of cattle, has made himself a small fortune in a relatively short space of time, and is now looking for a wife. And if you tell me you didn't know all that I won't believe you.'

'So I won't tell you.' Charlotte lifted her shoulders. 'In any case you'll only believe what you want to believe.' She set off again at a sharp pace and did not speak until they reached Tarnside. But she hated the idea that Rohan thought she was interested in Jonathan purely for the sake of his bank balance and knew she had to say something in her own defence.

'Jonathan didn't tell me he actually owned the ranch,' she said as she put her key in the door.

'Really?' It was obvious by his tone that he did not believe her.

'It's the truth; ask him yourself.'

'The man's a boaster,' he returned dismissively; 'he tells everyone. Don't try and pull the wool over my eyes, Charlotte; it won't work.'

She turned as the door opened, her eyes blazing, anger erupting from every pore in her body. 'You really are a bastard, aren't you? You believe what you want to believe and nothing I can say will change it; but one day you'll find out that you're mistaken, that I'm not the sort of girl you think I am. And when that day comes don't think I'll accept your apologies, because I won't.'

His laughter was harsh. 'If that day comes then I will apologise unreservedly.' But his voice told her that he did not think it would ever reach that point. 'What are we doing standing here on the doorstep? Let me see you inside.'

Charlotte shook her head firmly. 'It's quite all right; I've been coming home on my own ever since Glen died. Please go back to the party.'

But he insisted on entering and immediately Charlotte wished she had been more adamant. He filled the house with his presence, she felt the air choking thick, and had never been more conscious of him.

She stood and watched as he walked around as though he had never seen the place before, looking deliberately at the original paintings she and Glen had bought—admittedly not by old masters, but ones which he had assured her would become of some value one day—at the figurines and vases, the exciting period furniture, everything chosen between them and with great care—Glen had been an expert on antiques and good at spotting bargains—and she knew exactly what thoughts were going through Rohan's mind.

'I'm tired,' she said pointedly.

His eyes narrowed. 'Is that an invitation to bed? Are you daring to try it on with me as well?'

Fury welled up in her and again she attempted to slap him satisfyingly across the cheek, but as before he was quicker and caught her wrist in a vice-like grip. When he grabbed her other wrist too and pulled her up against him she thought he was going to kiss her, but suddenly, surprisingly, a mask came over his face. Every single feeling was shut away. He let her go and turned and walked out of the house.

CHAPTER THREE

NOT surprisingly Charlotte found difficulty in sleeping that night; she could not rid her mind of Rohan, and the thought of having to work side by side with him again on Monday brought her fresh anxiety. For as long as he continued to distrust her there would be no peace between them, and as the chance of him changing his mind was distinctly remote, if not an impossibility, there was little hope for the future.

Saturday proved an uneventful day filled with shopping, cleaning and washing and by evening she was totally exhausted, going to bed early, dropping straight off to sleep, making up for her wakefulness the night before.

On Sunday she was up early, going for a jog before breakfast and mid-morning when the telephone rang she was surprised to hear Rohan's deep voice. It was the first time he had ever rung her.

'My father is asking for you,' he said gruffly. 'He's not well; the doctor has confined him to bed and——'

'I'll be right there,' cut in Charlotte at once, her heart beating uneasily. Ever since Glen's death Douglas had suffered a heart murmur and she was afraid now that the excitement of his party had been too much for him.

She put the phone down without saying another word and ran all the way to Frenchwood Manor. She thought Rohan would be waiting for her; instead she had to bang on the door and wait for Douglas's housekeeper to let her in. Mrs Kirkland was plump and always pleasant but today her face was lined with worry. 'You know where his room is, don't you, dear?' she asked quietly.

Charlotte nodded and bounded up the stairs. Rohan met her outside his father's room. She ignored him, moving inside, expecting to see her father-in-law lying pale and weak against the pillows, surprised that he was sitting up, looking ready to do battle.

'Ah, good, Charlie, you've come. I don't know why the damn doctor insisted I stay in bed; it's driving me insane. Come and talk to me. Rohan, leave us alone for a while. This girl's like a breath of fresh air.'

'You know the doctor said not to overdo it, Father.' Rohan looked distinctly disapproving. 'You're supposed to be resting.'

'I am resting, dammit,' replied the older man tetchily. 'I've been in bed all day. Good lord, I'm not that ill.'

Rohan unwillingly left the room and Charlotte sat on the edge of the bed and took Douglas's hand. 'Why didn't you let me know earlier? What happened? Did you have another heart attack?'

'I guess I did,' he agreed reluctantly; 'and Rohan wouldn't let me send for you, said I needed my rest. Damn him, he's as bad as the doctor.'

Charlotte smiled and squeezed his hand. 'You're a crotchety old man, of course you need to rest, but I'm glad I'm here. If there's anything at all I can do just——'

'All I want is your company,' he interjected with a wry smile. 'You do me good, Charlie.' He was the only person ever to call her Charlie and Charlotte liked it, she felt it was a term of endearment, and the first time he had used it she knew that he had accepted her as a member of their family. There were certainly no feelings on his part that she was a gold-digger.

They sat talking, mainly about the party and how much he had enjoyed it, and inevitably they spoke about Glen, but gradually Douglas grew weary and lay back against the pillows and when Rohan returned he insisted she leave his father to sleep.

'I'll be back later,' she promised.

Charlotte headed straight for the front door and was thunderstruck when Rohan suddenly said, 'Why don't you stay for lunch?'

She turned and looked into the intent greyness of his eyes. 'Stay for lunch?'

His lips tried to smile but failed. 'That's right; Millie always cooks more than enough.'

'You're inviting *me* to have lunch with you?' She could not keep the incredulity out of her voice.

'My father wants to see you again later,' he pointed out. 'There's no point in running backwards and forwards.'

Charlotte shook her head. 'No, thank you; it's not far. I'd prefer that than put up with your company more than I have to.'

Rohan's lips tightened. 'I insist. The second my father wakes he will want to see you.'

'For Douglas's sake, then, I'll stay,' she agreed reluctantly, and followed him into the dining-room. On other occasions when she had eaten here with Glen and his father she had been thoroughly relaxed; today was a different story. Rohan did not want her here, she did not want to stay—it was a recipe for disaster.

'I wish you'd told me about your father earlier,' she said, accepting the glass of wine he offered.

'What could you have done?' asked Rohan with some asperity. 'He's slept a lot of the time; otherwise he's been like a bear with a sore head.'

'He seemed all right to me,' said Charlotte.

Rohan's lips twisted in a gesture of distaste. 'Naturally—because he's as besotted with you as Glen was. I'll hand you this, Charlotte McAulay, you're a very clever woman.'

'Will you stop calling me McAulay?' Her eyes were bright on his, her whole demeanour defensive.

'I don't like to think of you as a Courtenay,' he answered levelly.

'That's too bad,' she snapped, 'because I am a Courtenay now, and there's nothing you can say or do to change it.' She finished her wine in one long swallow and silently Rohan refilled her glass.

'Lunch is ready.' Millie Kirkland came bustling in with two bowls of steaming soup, and they took their seats at the table.

The conversation did not end there. As soon as he had taken his first spoonful Rohan said tersely, 'Are you suggesting that, as a Courtenay, you have a right to a say in the affairs of the company?'

'I don't see why not,' Charlotte answered. 'I know as much about Courtenay Textiles as Glen ever did, and definitely more than you.' It was the wrong thing to say but she did not care. He was so pompous he needed taking down a peg or two.

Rohan's eyes narrowed, 'Are you by any chance suggesting that you consider yourself a fit person actually to run it?'

Charlotte did not have to speak—her answer was there in her eyes for him to see.

'Just as I thought,' he rasped. 'Does my father know that you have such great aspirations?'

She shook her head.

'Then I suggest you keep them to yourself.'

'You mean *you* wouldn't give me the chance,' she flashed, 'and you're going to make sure Douglas doesn't either?'

'Precisely. Lord, do you think I'm an idiot? Do you think I don't know what your next step would be?' His grey eyes were cold and condemning.

'My next step?' asked Charlotte, frowning faintly. 'What are you talking about? What next step?'

He looked at her icily. 'Do you mean to say you wouldn't want to claim shares? That you wouldn't insist on some sort of financial deal?'

'I refuse to answer such a stupid question,' she cried furiously.

Brows lifted. 'It would appear I've hit the nail on the head.'

'I'm not after anything for myself,' she defended loudly. 'I want to help Douglas, that's all.'

'And I'm expected to believe that?'

Her blue eyes flamed. 'I know you'll never believe a word I say, but it happens to be the truth. I enjoy working at Courtenay's; I always have.'

'You're right, I don't believe you,' he replied. 'I'm not like Glen, you know; he was too easygoing for his own good. You duped him completely.'

What was the point in continuing to argue? Rohan would believe only what he wanted to believe. She broke off a piece of bread and popped it into her mouth, spooning her excellent asparagus soup, trying to ignore him. It was an impossibility. He was not the type you could ever ignore—his presence was too overwhelming. He could walk into a room while your back was turned and you would know instantly he was there without even looking.

'So, now you know that you're never likely to be put in charge, exactly what are your plans?' he asked, after they had both finished their soup in, as far as Charlotte was concerned, uncomfortable silence.

Charlotte clamped her lips together as she looked at him, her eyes warring with his for several long seconds before she answered. 'Whatever I say my plans are you're sure to try and thwart them.'

'Indeed. My advice to you, after we have set the business back on its feet—which might prove difficult considering the amount of lower-priced imports that are flooding the country these days—would be to sell up and start afresh somewhere else.'

'It would hurt your father if I left,' she retorted. To say nothing of her own feelings. She had had three happy years at Tarnside with Glen, not exciting, not exhilarating, but happy enough in their own way, and she did not want to move. This was her home now and she wanted to stay.

'I wouldn't stop you coming to see him now and then.'

The gall of the man! Charlotte sat up straight in her chair and eyed him furiously across the table. 'How magnanimous of you.' Her tone was filled with scorn. 'You'll be saying next that you'll even find me somewhere else to live.'

He inclined his head. 'I actually know a perfect little——'

She stopped him with an out-thrust hand, shaking her head in horror. 'You are, without a doubt, the most unbelievable person I've ever met. I don't think I want any more food; I feel sick.' She pushed her chair back. 'Give Mrs Kirkland my apologies; I'll be back later to see your father.'

But she did not make it to the door. He was there before her, halting her progress, an enigmatic smile on his lips, a dangerous glitter to his eyes. 'I didn't class you as the type to run away, Charlotte.'

'What am I, then? The type to take whatever you care to dish out?' she flashed furiously. 'Glen always said you took after your father, but, heavens, you're nothing like him. Douglas has never treated me with anything other than courtesy. You're the biggest swine I've ever met or ever want to meet; but I'll tell you this, Rohan Courtenay, you're not driving me out of my house, whatever you say or do.'

Millie Kirkland chose that moment to come in with dishes of hot vegetables and to take away their empty soup bowls, and she looked surprised to see them standing there by the door.

'Sit down,' Rohan muttered harshly when his father's housekeeper had gone again, 'and stop making a fool of yourself.'

'Only if you promise to stop harassing me,' she hissed.

'You get upset too easily.'

'Wouldn't anyone, in the face of such insults?' she cried. 'I'm sure I don't know what I've done to deserve any of it. My only crime, it would appear, was in marrying your brother. I'm sorry you didn't approve.'

His eyes flayed her with their intensity. 'That's only the half of it. According to Glen even your marriage was experiencing difficulties. Proof yet again that you only wanted him for one thing, that love never entered into it.'

Charlotte's mouth dropped open in complete and utter astonishment. What was he talking about now? 'Glen couldn't possibly have said that; there was nothing wrong with our marriage.'

'Oh, but he did,' Rohan returned coldly, and then, as the housekeeper entered the room again, 'Ah, Millie, roast beef, my favourite.'

'And plenty of Yorkshire pudding,' she added with a fond smile, and to Charlotte, 'This man could live on Yorkshire pudding and gravy.'

Charlotte liked it herself. During these last few months she had not eaten properly, not having the heart to cook a meal for one, and had actually been looking forward to her lunch—until Rohan had astounded her with his suggestion that she had been having troubles with her marriage.

'I want to know exactly what Glen said,' Charlotte stated once the woman had left.

Rohan lifted his shoulders in an expressive shrug. 'No more than I've already told you. He didn't like being continually pestered for money and was afraid it would affect your marriage——'

'Liar!' cut in Charlotte fiercely. 'I never asked Glen for a penny. I earned a good wage myself; I didn't need to ask for more. If he wanted to spend money on me then that was something different altogether. But he could never say that I asked for any. You're making it up; you're trying to discredit me even further.'

Rohan continued to chew his beef.

'Answer me, dammit,' she cried.

His brows lifted, eyes looked steadily at her. 'It's the truth.'

Charlotte sagged in her seat; what was the point? It was like trying to pit herself against a brick wall. She picked up her knife and sliced a potato in half, but she did not put any into her mouth. The thought of food suddenly choked her.

'Stop being foolish and eat,' he said suddenly. 'Millie will be offended if you leave your meal untouched.'

And so she tried, but it tasted like sawdust, and she knew that the sooner she could get out of here the better. Rohan still had to be lying; Glen would never have said something like that. Would he? Their marriage had lacked the sort of spark that had existed between her and Rohan, but she had thought he was happy enough. Surely he would have said if he'd had any complaints?

The atmosphere grew so thick that Charlotte knew she had to talk about something completely different. If not she would go out of her mind. 'I can't stand this,' she said. 'Can we talk about the weather, or world affairs, or even about you? Yes, tell me about yourself. You live in London and run a multi-national concern and that's as much as I know.'

'I didn't realise you were interested.' Grey eyes rested on hers.

'I'm not particularly,' she told him, 'but I'm fed up with being the main topic of conversation. How did you manage to reach such a position at your age?'

'Damned hard work,' he told her. 'It didn't drop into my lap.'

Which was another dig at her, Charlotte realised, and it took all her will-power not to retaliate. 'So how did you actually start?' she asked. 'And why didn't you join your father?'

'Because I thought weaving woollen material, or any material for that matter, was dreadfully dull, and I could see its decline approaching. I wanted to be part of a young and growing industry.'

'So you went into computers and now sell your microchips all over the world?'

He inclined his head. 'Something like that. It's big business.'

'But it couldn't have been easy to start with.'

'Is any business? I did a course at college and then became a computer programmer, but that was too easy—so I became a computer analyser—but then I got more interested in how things were made than putting them right. I started my own small company and it grew from there.'

He made it sound simple but Charlotte knew that he had worked long and hard hours. His entrepeneurial spirit had certainly paid off. According to Glen his brother was a millionaire many times over.

'How long do you intend staying here?'

He smiled, though it held no real pleasure. 'It all depends how long it takes to put Courtenay Textiles back on its feet. I do, however, have every faith that nothing will go wrong with my own business while I'm away.'

Not for the first time Charlotte wished that she had not ignored the company completely while Glen was ill. Although she did not entirely blame herself for its decline, she perhaps could have done something to stop it, have seen what was happening. If only Douglas hadn't told her to take as much time off as she liked. If only she hadn't put Eric Shotton in charge. If only, if only. It was a relatively small mill but it would be a shame if it was allowed to go out of business after all these years.

'You look disappointed, Charlotte.'

'Of course I am.'

'You still think you could do the job yourself?'

'Yes, I do, as a matter of fact.'

'I hope you're not thinking of telling my father that. I don't want him involved in any of this.'

'Douglas has always shown a great interest in the company,' she retorted. 'Glen used to give him daily reports, and I'm sure that if I asked him he'd be only too pleased to let me take over. He must know I'm capable.'

'Capable of milking some of the profits as well,' he retorted.

Charlotte gasped. 'How dare you?'

To her astonishment he suddenly smiled. 'You're beautiful when you're angry.'

'And you're a swine,' she snapped.

Apple pie and custard followed the beef. It was a delicious, well-cooked meal and Charlotte would have enjoyed it had it not been for Rohan's attitude. It was not a nice feeling to be condemned when you were innocent. But somehow, some way she would prove that he was wrong; she was not going to live the rest of her life with this unfounded accusation hanging over her head.

They lapsed into silence and when they finished their meal Rohan suggested they take their coffee out into the garden. It was a lovely warm day in the middle of May and she welcomed the suggestion.

The atmosphere in the room had become claustrophobic and she needed to fill her lungs with fresh air, to breathe without feeling Rohan in every pore. He was, without a doubt, a man who could not easily be dismissed, but outdoors she would certainly stand a better chance.

She ignored the white chairs on the patio, taking her cup and wandering through the grounds. She had fallen in love with Frenchwood Manor the first time she set eyes on it; it was everything she had ever coveted. Not, she told herself quickly, that that was the reason she had married Glen. But she had had so little as a child, living in a tiny terraced house where there was no privacy, feeling hurt by the lack of affection from her parents. It had been like another world. And now this man was spoiling things, making unjust accusations, and she hated him for it and intended fighting him every inch of the way.

His padded footsteps on the grass behind her warned of his approach and Charlotte felt every hair prickle on the back of her neck. She had hoped to escape, had wanted a few moments alone to gather her thoughts. What did he want now?

'Are you trying to run away from me, Charlotte?' He spoke before he even reached her.

She turned and looked at him coolly. 'Why should I do that?'

He lifted his shoulders. 'You tell me.'

'I simply wanted to stretch my legs.'

'You could have drunk your coffee on the patio and we could have walked together.'

Charlotte eyed him dispassionately. 'I felt like being alone.'

'In other words, yes, you were running away. Did a few home truths hurt? Is that what's wrong?'

'Everything about you is wrong,' she countered hotly. 'Will you please keep away from me?' She swung around so quickly that she spilled the coffee from her cup and with a cry of anger she threw the rest away and then thrust the cup and saucer at Rohan. 'I've finished with this, you can take it back, and I'd be obliged if you'd allow me to continue my walk alone.'

Her sudden attack surprised him. He took the china but instead of returning to the patio he placed it on a bench a few feet away by the fish pond and rejoined Charlotte. 'I meant what I said earlier about you looking beautiful when you're angry. Your blue eyes are very bright, your cheeks glow, and you look very, very enticing. Did Glen ever see you like this?'

'No, he didn't,' she snapped. 'Glen and I never argued.'

'This isn't what he told me.'

She knew Rohan was goading her and yet she could not stop herself from retaliating. 'You're a liar. He was a wonderful, wonderful husband, and there was nothing wrong with our marriage. Just go away, will you, and stop trying to goad me?'

Again she marched ahead of him and again he caught her up; but this time he was not content with conversation alone. He caught her arm and spun her to face him; their eyes met in a mutual blazing battle, she felt her heart thunder with both anger and something verging on excitement, and the next second his mouth captured hers.

Guilt immediately flooded through her and Charlotte knew she had to free herself, and do it immediately for her own peace of mind. It was wrong to feel even a spark of desire so soon after Glen's death, and more shameful still that it was his own brother arousing these emotions. But when she wriggled her hands up between them and pushed against his chest he merely laughed harshly and carried on kissing her.

His body was hard, his arms strong, and she felt a fierce surge of unwanted desire spiral up from the pit of her stomach. Lord, she hated herself for it, and nothing, she vowed savagely, nothing at all would make her submit; she had no intention of giving in to a chemical attraction that would riddle her with guilt for the rest of her life.

She kicked and struggled and made angry sounds in the back of her throat—but as the kiss went on and on in spite of her struggles Charlotte knew she was fighting a losing battle. Every ounce of desire they had both fought against in years gone by was emerging in full dynamic force.

CHAPTER FOUR

THE hammer-beats of Rohan's heart rang in unison with Charlotte's and she was totally devastated that such a thing could be happening to her, that he could arouse her so unwittingly, that her feelings for Glen could be pushed so shockingly to the back of her mind.

She hated herself for her weakness and continued to fight Rohan like a wildcat for long minute following long minute, and eventually, painfully, an eternity later, she was free.

Immediately she put space between them, her chest heaving, her legs oddly weak, her expression both angry and defiant. 'You beast! You swine! I hate you.'

Rohan's laughter was deep and loud. 'I'll give you credit for putting up a strong fight.'

'I'll do more than that if you ever try to kiss me again,' she cried. 'What game do you think you're playing?'

'I told you, you're irresistible when you're angry.' Still his amusement persisted.

'And you thought you'd take advantage?' she demanded, her whole body as taut as a tightly wound watch-spring. 'Well let me tell you this, Rohan Courtenay: I do not want your kisses, I will not allow your kisses, and I demand that you let me finish my walk alone. I find your company totally abhorrent.'

She swung on her heel and headed in the direction of the woods. She refused to look back but could not hear him following, although that was not to say he wasn't; he could tread as softly as a panther if he wanted to. However, there were no tell-tale prickles to her spine, and if she could trust her own feelings it meant that she was alone at last.

The lawn sloped away from the house, past the well-stocked fish pond and the shrubbery until it came to the beech woods. Charlotte found its cool shade welcome and she forged on until she felt safe and then leaned back against the bole of a tree, her hands behind her touching the coarse texture of the bark.

Despite the fact that she had fought and kicked and told Rohan that she hated him her body was telling her a different story. Her heart was not pounding from exertion but because of the extreme feelings he had managed to arouse; her body was not warm because she had been hurrying but because of the heat of her desire.

All those years she had quenched these feelings, thought they were finally dead, and now, when she least expected them, when she did not want them, they had returned with a vengeance. What disturbed her more was that she had never felt like this where Glen was concerned; their loving had been gentle, lacking in fire of any sort, and yet she had never doubted for one second that she did love him. She felt a very real sense of disquiet.

And the irony of the whole situation was that Rohan's feelings for her had changed completely. His desire before had been mingled with very real attraction; now it was tempered with loathing and distrust, and maybe even a sense of revenge! She got the feeling that he wanted to hurt her.

How long she stood there Charlotte did not know, but when she eventually decided to return to the house she could not believe her eyes when she found Rohan sitting on the bench by the pool waiting for her.

'I was about to come and see if you'd got lost,' he said pleasantly, pushing himself to his feet.

'How could I get lost when I know the woods so well?' she questioned, her tone bitter. 'Glen and I often used to walk there.'

'And was it Glen you were thinking about now?' He walked by her side and Charlotte felt her senses leap in response and guessed it would always be like this. She could only hope and pray that she would never give herself away, that she would be able to keep her feelings and her guilt well-hidden until such time as he went back to London.

'Naturally,' she answered.

'I did not enter your thoughts?'

'Oh, yes, I thought about you as well,' she assured him. 'But they weren't pleasant thoughts, and if I were you I wouldn't ask what they were.'

'I guess you were thinking what a detestable swine I am,' he said, not looking in the least put out, 'that you hate my guts, and that you're not going to let me touch you ever again.'

Charlotte eyed him coldly and dispassionately, but inside she was alarmed that he had read her mind so accurately.

'But the truth is, Charlotte, that even though you tell yourself you don't want my kisses you enjoy them. You actually want me as much as I want you. Deny it if you dare.'

'I do deny it,' lied Charlotte fiercely. 'Maybe I used to feel attracted to you, many years ago, but do you really think nothing has changed after all the things you've said, all the accusations you've made? You're the last man on earth I want to let anywhere near me, and you'd best remember that.' Her blue eyes flashed, her whole body rejecting him.

'There are some things we can do nothing about.' Still his lips quirked.

Charlotte stamped her foot angrily. 'I'm not that lacking in will-power, Rohan Courtenay, and if you had any thoughts at all for your brother then you'd leave me alone.'

A shadow crossed his face, but he was not stopped in his pursuit of her. 'You do admit that you feel something?'

'No, I do not,' she stated fiercely. 'Do you really think I'd be so disloyal to Glen?'

'I wouldn't call it disloyal. There has always been a spark of attraction between us. I think even Glen knew that.'

Charlotte sniffed disdainfully, disbelievingly. 'I think you're out of your mind and I see no point in continuing this conversation. I'm going back to see Douglas and then I'm going home.' She did not even look at Rohan again, storming off in front of him, wishing with all her heart that he would leave her alone.

Douglas looked pleased to see them both. 'Where have you been? I've been waiting for you.'

'We've been walking our lunch off in the garden,' answered Rohan.

'The fresh air has certainly put some colour in your cheeks, Charlie,' asserted her father-in-law, looking at her fondly, and then to Rohan, 'How long do you think the damn doctor's going to keep me here? I want to get up; I can't stand the inactivity.'

'It's for your own good,' said Charlotte softly before Rohan could answer. She sat on the edge of the bed again and took his hand. 'The more you rest now, the more quickly you'll get better.'

'Hmmph!' he snorted. 'I feel fit enough. It was nothing. Rohan panicked and sent for the doctor, but there's nothing wrong with me that a few hours in bed hasn't put right. It was just the party; I stayed up too late, that's all.'

'We'll see what tomorrow brings,' said Rohan. 'Dr Scott is calling in again then.'

Douglas continued to grumble, Charlotte tried to placate, and Rohan stood and watched. Eventually, when her father-in-law seemed to grow weary, she took her leave, promising to come back again to see him before she went to work the next morning.

'You'll ring me if there's any change?' she asked Rohan anxiously as he accompanied her to the front door.

He inclined his head, his eyes ever watchful on hers. Charlotte felt uncomfortable and hastened away without saying another word.

Back at Tarnside she flopped into a chair and closed her eyes. What a day! Douglas's unexpected and worrying illness, Rohan's suggestion that Glen hadn't been happy in their marriage, and, perhaps even more disturbing, Rohan's kiss and her reaction to it.

Where Rohan had got the idea that Glen hadn't been happy she did not know. There had not been one thing wrong with their marriage—not that she was aware of, anyway—and surely Glen would have said if there was anything bothering him? Maybe they hadn't been the most fiery and innovative of lovers but they had been the best of friends, comfortable in each other's company, able to discuss openly anything and everything that they were feeling. She shook her head. Rohan had to be wrong.

But he wasn't wrong in his suggestion that she wanted him as much as he wanted her. It was a frightening thought, and the way he had behaved today indicated that he wouldn't be backward at coming forward. She would really have to be on her guard, keeping a very tight rein on her own emotions. It was truly an unsettling situation.

When the telephone rang an hour later Charlotte immediately assumed Douglas's condition had worsened, but when she picked up the receiver she did not recognise the male voice at the other end. It was certainly not Rohan.

'Who is this?' she asked sharply.

'Jonathan Herald; don't you remember me?'

She closed her eyes and gave a silent groan. 'I'm sorry; yes, of course I remember you. I wasn't expecting to hear from you, that's all.'

'I said I'd be in touch,' he answered, sounding hurt. 'I wondered if you'd like to go out for a drink? I've thought about nothing but you ever since Friday night.'

'I'm sorry, I'm tired,' she excused herself. 'I've been out all day.'

'Yes, I know, I rang earlier. How about tomorrow night, then?'

Charlotte did not want to go out with Jonathan tomorrow night or any night. He had proved an effective shield against Rohan, but he was far too bluff and hearty for her to gain any real pleasure out of dating him. 'I'm sorry, Jonathan, I don't want to hurt your feelings but I don't want to go out with you.'

'Is there someone else?'

'No,' she answered, 'no one else.'

'In that case there's hope,' he answered cheerfully.

When she finally put down the phone Charlotte was startled when it rang again straight away.

This time it was Rohan and immediately her thoughts fled to Douglas. 'Is something wrong?' she asked breathlessly.

'You were engaged,' he accused. 'Who were you talking to?'

She found his audacity astonishing. 'My private life has nothing to do with you.'

'It wouldn't have been Jonathan Herald by any chance?'

Her mouth fell open. 'What are you, a mind-reader?'

'Then it was Jonathan?'

'Yes, as a matter of fact. How did you know?'

'He rang to see if you were here. He seems very taken with you, Charlotte. You must have given him a lot of encouragement.'

'I've told him I don't want to see him,' she answered explosively.

'And I'm expected to believe that?'

'I doubt you will.'

'The man has money, Charlotte; he's your type.'

'And so have you,' she claimed impatiently; 'that would supposedly make you my type as well. But as a matter of fact neither of you is. Is this why you've phoned, to question me about Jonathan, or is your father worse?'

'He's no worse,' he assured her; 'still cranky, still insisting he's well enough to get up.'

'In that case, there's nothing more we have to say,' Charlotte announced, and slammed down the receiver.

The gall of the man, checking up on her like that. And the cheek of Jonathan, ringing the Courtenay house. They both angered her for different reasons and if she ever saw Jonathan again she would give him a piece of her mind.

The rest of the day was uneventful in comparison and she went to bed early, though not to sleep. Tomorrow she had to face Rohan again, had to work by his side, and the thought of it was totally abhorrent. He seemed to treat her as his slave rather than an equal. It was nothing like the working relationship she had had with

Glen and she thoroughly hated it, and if it weren't for the fact that she cared about the company, that she knew things no one else did and was of considerable help to Rohan, she would definitely have steered clear of the whole place.

At eight-fifteen Charlotte called at Frenchwood Manor. Douglas's housekeeper let her in and the woman's cheerful face was proof that her employer was feeling better. 'The doctor's already been,' she said, 'and given him permission to get up. But he's to go back to bed the instant he feels tired, not that I can see him doing that. I'll have to watch him like a hawk.'

'You do that, Millie,' said Charlotte. 'Is he up and dressed now? Can I see him?'

'He's in the dining-room eating his breakfast; Rohan too; go on in, I'm sure they won't mind. Have you eaten? Would you like me to cook you——?'

'Thank you, Millie, but no,' countered Charlotte at once. 'I've had some toast.'

She paused in the doorway to the dining-room, seeing the two men who were so much alike sitting eating their breakfast. Douglas looked remarkably well but it was Rohan who saw her first.

'You have a visitor, Father,' he announced, and his eyes seemed to rake her whole body, not missing one inch, causing a flood of unwanted warmth to spread through her limbs.

'Ah, Charlie, my dear, come in, come in,' said the older man, smiling widely.

'You're looking well,' she said, ignoring Rohan completely.

'I am well, child, completely recovered. Won't you join us? It won't take Millie long to——'

She shook her head. 'I simply wanted to check you were all right before I went to work. I can see you are, so I'll be——'

'You may as well wait for Rohan and go together,' Douglas broke in before she could finish. 'Have some coffee at least. There's a pot full here that will only go to waste. Come and sit by me.'

Charlotte was given no choice, but opposite her sat Rohan and the sudden hardness in his eyes made it clear that he did not like the easy camaraderie she had with his father. He obviously still thought she was pandering up to him for his money. She glared back.

Douglas continued to talk cheerfully, either unaware of the atmosphere or deliberately ignoring it, and as soon as Rohan finished eating he declared himself ready. Charlotte hugged the older man and kissed him warmly on the cheek, promising to call in again that evening.

For the first five minutes they drove in complete silence, Charlotte's hands tightly clasped on her lap, her eyes straight ahead, trying to ignore Rohan at her side. It was impossible. His sensuality came across in waves so strong, they threatened to overwhelm her; yesterday's unwanted kiss returned to haunt her, her whole body felt as though it was on fire, and no matter how much she told herself that such feelings were wrong she could not stop them.

'Something tells me you're not happy this morning.'

Rohan's voice, breaking into her thoughts, made her look at him sharply. 'I've not been happy since you took over.' Her tone was defiant; it helped to take refuge in anger. 'I don't like the way you've assumed responsibility for the company when you previously wanted nothing to do with it.'

'It's not my fault it's going through a bad time,' he replied calmly.

'And it's not my fault Glen became ill,' she retaliated. 'It's unfair to accuse me of being the cause of Courtenay's downfall.'

'I don't think it is unfair.' He glanced across at her as he stopped at a set of traffic lights, dark brows rising mockingly. 'I think Glen was so infatuated, he let you have your own way, not realising that your motives were less than honourable.'

'How dare you?' Charlotte was beside herself with rage. 'You know nothing. You're making it up just because of some perverted notion that all I'm interested in is rich men. You're depraved, Rohan Courtenay.'

His mouth twitched. 'I only know what I see and hear.'

'Giving everything your own interpretation,' she slammed. 'Did you speak to Barry? Did you ask him exactly why I ended our engagement?'

The lights changed and the Jaguar moved forward. 'I didn't need to; I found out what I wanted to know from other sources.'

'What sources?' she demanded.

'Does that matter?' he asked. 'Let it suffice that I was satisfied with what I was told.'

Charlotte wondered whom he had spoken to. Bernadette, the woman with whom Barry had been unfaithful? Or Bernadette's husband? It had been a tangled, destructive affair and neither one of them would have had a good word to say.

She shook her head, red hair flying, trying to dismiss such unwanted thoughts from her mind. Rohan was an impossible man, causing pain by raking up the past, casting aspersions on her character, suggesting her marriage had been a sham, making it impossible for her to think clearly yet alone work alongside him.

There were times when Charlotte wished she had a close friend she could confide in. Her best friend from schooldays also worked at Courtenay Textiles and they had always spent their lunch breaks together—until Charlotte married the boss. Then things had changed. Jacqui hadn't wanted to know her and some of the other employees too had distinctly cooled towards her. She guessed they thought the same as Rohan.

It hadn't really bothered her at the time because she'd had Glen, but now she really did wish that she had a confidante, someone with whom she could talk things over, decide what her best plan of action would be.

Once they arrived she took off her jacket and filled the kettle with water. Rohan liked a continuous supply of coffee throughout the morning. Her office adjoined Glen's—as she still preferred to think it—and as she waited for the water to boil she could hear Rohan on the telephone—and it was obviously not a business call.

Charlotte could not hear distinctly what was being said but she caught the name Merelda and wondered who had called whom. Perhaps Rohan had arranged to see his cousin yesterday and had been compelled to postpone their date when his father was taken ill. Perhaps he was ringing to fix another time.

When his voice went too low to hear anything she could only assume that he was whispering words of endearment, and to her own annoyance Charlotte felt a sudden stab of jealousy. It was stupid, she knew, and yet she could not help it. Heavens, she did not want to feel anything for this man, she hated and resented him, so why feel jealous over his interest in another woman?

Was it the thought that when he kissed Merelda the girl felt the same surge of awareness that she herself felt, the same sort of response? Except that Merelda would have no hesitation in returning his kiss, would hold nothing back, would give as good as she got and——

Charlotte suddenly realised that Rohan had finished his call, left his office and walked into hers—and she was sitting staring into space. She grew suddenly warm.

'Is there a problem?' he asked crisply.

'I'm waiting for the kettle to boil.'

'Then I suggest you go and check.'

His tone was harsh and Charlotte wondered whether she had been wrong; whether, after all, his conversation with Merelda hadn't been as sweet as she thought. Perhaps the girl had been angry with him for letting her down? Whatever, it was not going to make her life any easier this morning.

File after file he demanded, lists to be drawn up, new systems to be considered, meetings arranged. No time for lunch, just a sandwich brought in and another pot of coffee. By the end of the day Charlotte's head was in a whirl and she began to think that he was doing it deliberately.

Ever since he had taken over he had been like a whirlwind, but today he was even worse—working her, pushing her, stressing her, until her head throbbed and her mind threatened to pack up.

Normally they finished at five; by six he showed no sign of calling a halt. It was probably because she was without transport, decided Charlotte, and he knew she could not go home until he was ready. He was testing her stamina. So she said nothing, carrying on with the jobs he detailed, and it was well past seven before he finally decided they had done enough.

They walked out of the silent offices together and got into his car. Charlotte's head still pounded and she felt so drained that she closed her eyes. The next thing she knew Rohan was touching her arm and telling her they were home.

She expected to find herself outside her own house, and was totally surprised to see Frenchwood Manor. 'What am I doing here?' she asked, trying to shake herself free of her lethargy.

'You look in no fit state to cook a meal.'

'I have a headache, that's all,' she told him tersely. 'I'm not intruding on you again.'

He shook his head impatiently. 'You promised to come back and see my father. He will be disappointed if you don't keep your word.'

She was given no choice, but once in the house Charlotte wished that she had been more adamant because waiting for Rohan in the lounge was none other than his beautiful cousin, Merelda.

'I came to see Uncle Douglas,' she purred, sidling up to Rohan the second he entered the hallway, taking his arm and rubbing herself against him, completely unaware of Charlotte trailing a few feet behind, 'and I invited myself to dinner at the same time; I hope you don't mind? I——' Suddenly she saw Charlotte and her mouth fell open. 'I didn't realise she would be here.'

'I've come to see my father-in-law too,' announced Charlotte firmly. Where is he, in the——?'

'He's in bed,' Merelda interjected, her green eyes narrowed and hostile.

'In that case,' said Charlotte, fearing he had had a turn for the worse, 'I'll go up and see him straight away.'

Douglas's eyes were closed but he sensed her presence as she crept into his bedroom and smiled weakly and guiltily. 'I think maybe I'm not as strong as I thought I was. Millie packed me off to bed an hour ago and to tell you the truth it's very welcome.'

'It's a good job someone's making you see sense,' she whispered fondly, bending to kiss his pale brow.

'You're staying for dinner?' he asked hoarsely.

Charlotte grimaced. 'Rohan did suggest it but as you're in bed I think I might go home. Besides, Merelda's here; I don't want to play gooseberry.'

'Gooseberry? With Merelda and Rohan?' He looked amused at the thought. 'They're cousins, childhood buddies, there's nothing between them...although I have to admit it's unfortunate she turned up. I would like you and Rohan to spend more time together.'

'We've done enough of that all day.' Charlotte was unable to keep the bitterness out of her voice.

'Yes, but that's work. Rohan is a different beast when he's working. I want you to spend time together socially, Charlie; I'm sure you'll see quite a different side to him then. I don't like to see my two favourite people at odds.'

'It's nothing new, Douglas,' she assured him; 'we've never particularly liked each other.'

He looked surprised. 'I didn't know that; you kept it well hidden. I thought it was something recent.'

'I pretended to like Rohan for Glen's sake,' she told him, 'but we're as different as chalk from cheese. You're fighting a losing battle trying to make us into friends. We'll never be that.'

'Charlotte's right, Father.'

They both looked in surprise at the doorway. Rohan filled it with his presence, a deep, angry frown scouring his brow, clearly disapproving of the fact that she had been discussing him with his father.

'Come in, son, come in,' said Douglas at once. 'Where's Merelda?'

'If you're hoping she's gone so that Charlotte and I can spend time on our own you're mistaken. She's downstairs with a gin and tonic.' There was an edge to his tone that he could not quite hide. 'How are you, Father, or do I need to ask? Charlotte seems to be doing a very good job of heaping troubles on your shoulders.'

Douglas looked at his son in surprise. 'She's being honest, son, which is what I want; I hate lies and deceitfulness.'

Charlotte's eyes caught Rohan's and she knew exactly what he was thinking, and she waited for the usual unfounded accusations, but none came. 'I'll go and join Merelda,' she said uncertainly.

Douglas looked at her and smiled. 'Come and see me later, child, before you go home. I'm sorry I can't be more company.'

Downstairs Charlotte sought Merelda out, not really wanting to spend time with her but good manners prevailing. The brunette eyed her fiercely and resentfully. 'I had no idea you and Rohan were so friendly.'

'We're not,' said Charlotte at once.

'He invited you back for dinner.' It was an accusation made in terse, distant tones.

'Only because I was coming to see my father-in-law anyway.'

'He didn't take his eyes off you at Douglas's party.'

Charlotte shrugged. 'That isn't my fault; but I can assure you that there's no love lost between us.'

Even as she uttered the words she wondered whether they were true. There were changes taking place inside her, changes that she did not like, that were disloyal to Glen and should be stamped on without further delay. Her physical awareness seemed to be changing into emotional awareness. She was desperately trying to deny it, trying to pretend it was hatred that filled her body, but—was that really true?

CHAPTER FIVE

THE evening was a complete disaster as far as Charlotte was concerned. Admittedly Rohan did not ignore her—he included her in the conversation at all times—but Merelda made it abundantly clear that she was intruding. Not in what she said—oh, no, she was much too clever for that—but if looks could kill Charlotte would have died a thousand times over.

Merelda sat at Rohan's side, Charlotte opposite them, therefore he could not see his cousin's expression when she threw damning looks in Charlotte's direction. She constantly put her hand on his arm, smiling with cloying sweetness into his face. This man is mine, she seemed to be saying; keep your hands off.

As soon as the meal ended Charlotte announced she was leaving, ignoring Rohan's start of surprise, running up to see Douglas once more and then letting herself out of the house. Rohan met her at the front door. 'I'll walk you home.'

'And what would Merelda have to say about that?' asked Charlotte coldly.

He lifted his shoulders. 'I'll be but a few minutes. Merelda won't mind waiting; she'll understand.'

Charlotte was not so sure. Although Merelda had cleverly hid her jealousy she had not liked Charlotte joining them one little bit. The girl had presumed she and Rohan would be alone, and it had angered her that his sister-in-law shared their table.

'Thank you for the offer, but no, thanks,' said Charlotte, keeping her tone crisp and cool. 'It's no distance; I'll be all right.' And without waiting for him to argue further she hurried away into the darkness.

She was not afraid; she had walked this path many, many times. It was private property, no one ever trespassed, visitors usually came by car, so she was perfectly safe; Rohan was worrying for nothing.

But when she got to Tarnside a strange car was parked outside, and as she drew closer a dark shape unfolded itself and stood waiting for her. Charlotte's heartbeats quickened and she wished now that she had accepted Rohan's offer. Glen had had a security light installed which came on when anyone approached, but the bulb had gone and she hadn't replaced it and so the whole area was in darkness. There wasn't even a moon.

And then came a voice. 'Charlotte, is that you?'

It was Jonathan! Although it was a relief to discover it was no stranger lurking, he was still not welcome. She'd had more than enough to cope with today without having to put up with this man as well. 'Yes, Jonathan. What are you doing here at this time of night?'

She could not hide the tetchiness in her voice. She still had her headache, she felt bad-tempered, and was looking forward to a long relaxing bath before going to bed.

'I was practically passing.' She drew close now and could make him out more clearly. 'So I thought I'd call in and see you.'

'For just one minute, then,' she said begrudgingly as she unlocked her front door. 'But I'm warning you, I'm ready for bed. I'm whacked; I've had a busy day.' She flicked a switch and the hall flooded with light.

'I did try to ring you earlier,' he explained, following her inside and closing the door behind him. 'Have you been somewhere nice?'

'Not unless you call working late at the office nice,' she countered dismissively, 'and I've been to see my father-in-law; he's not very well.' She deliberately kept her tone unwelcoming. 'You had no right ringing there last night; it was completely out of order. I'd be obliged if you don't do it again.'

'I'm sorry,' he said, but it didn't sound as though he meant it.

'So am I,' she returned crisply. 'Would you like a cup of coffee? And then I must insist that you leave.' It was an offer made from pure politeness, not because she wanted to spend any time with him. He was making a nuisance of himself and she wished to goodness he would realise it.

'I'd love one,' he answered, following her into the oak-fitted kitchen that was her pride and joy. 'Mmm, nice place you have here; you must be feeling very lonely these days.'

'I've learned to cope,' said Charlotte, her voice intentionally sharp. If he was suggesting she needed company—*his* company—then he was very much mistaken. 'Will instant do?'

'Anything,' he said easily. 'Have you thought again about coming out with me?'

'You're a very persistent man, Jonathan Herald.' She filled the kettle and switched it on, reaching out cups and saucers, hoping she was not going to regret inviting him in.

He grinned, sublimely unaware that she was harbouring such harsh thoughts. 'Guilty as accused. I've learned that if you want something in this life you have to go out and get it. If I wait I might lose you.'

Charlotte frowned swiftly. 'Lose me? That's a rather ambiguous statement, isn't it? You can't lose what you haven't got.'

'You know what I mean,' he said with an easy shrug of his well-muscled shoulders, a disarming grin on his rugged face. 'You're a very attractive woman, Charlotte, you must have been told that many times, and some other man's going to snap you up if I don't get in first.'

She shook her head impatiently, trying her hardest to hide her anger. 'I've told you, I'm not interested in dating anyone yet. You're wasting your time.'

'I'll be going back to Texas shortly.'

And I won't miss you one iota, she thought.

'I was hoping that—well, this might come as a surprise, but I think I'm in love with you, Charlotte, and I thought that you might come——'

'*In love with me*?' she countered incredulously. 'You have to be joking; you don't even know me. I heard you were looking for a wife to take back to your ranch but this is ridiculous.' And she definitely wished now that she had not invited him in. He looked like being very persistent—*too* persistent; he was going to take a lot of handling. Rohan's warning rang loud in her ears.

'Don't you believe in love at first sight?' His voice was as hearty as ever, not at all the sort of tones one used when speaking of love. She could not imagine him having a true romantic streak in his whole body.

'No, I don't,' she said firmly. 'I believe you need to get to know a person really well before you can decide whether you love them or not. First feelings are usually purely sexual. And if that's what you feel for me then I'm afraid you'll be disappointed. Didn't I make myself clear on the telephone?'

He heaved a resigned sigh. 'Is it Glen's brother you're interested in?'

'Rohan?' she ejaculated. 'Not on your life.'

'He's a good catch.'

She frowned. Why did everybody bring it down to money? 'Maybe, but I'm not interested; not in Rohan, not in you, not in any man. Do you take sugar?'

'Yes, please, two. Is he interested in you?' His green eyes watched her closely.

'Heavens, no.' Charlotte gave a short, sharp laugh. 'He has Merelda; she's there with him now. Rohan and I have nothing at all in common. We're working together, but that's all. Here, put your own milk in.' She was fast losing patience with Jonathan.

He appeared oblivious to her hostility, perching himself on a stool at the breakfast-bar, sipping his coffee, looking at her with undiluted admiration. 'I'm not going to give up, Charlotte.'

She heaved a sigh and looked at him sadly. 'If I gave the wrong impression at Douglas's party, I'm sorry, Jonathan. What do I have to say to prove to you that I'm not interested?'

'Women always change their minds,' he told her easily; 'it's part of their charm. This is delicious coffee, by the way.'

It was a good three-quarters of an hour later before he finally left, all Charlotte's hints that she was deadly tired and wanted to go to bed falling on deaf ears. He was intent only on persuading her to go out with him.

Once she was alone Charlotte put their cups in the dishwasher, took some aspirin, soaked in the bath, and it was well after eleven before she climbed wearily into bed. When her alarm went off at seven-thirty the next morning she groaned and rolled over on to her other side, wishing she did not have to get up and go to work.

Never, in the whole of her career, had she wished that. She had always enjoyed her job; now it was an effort to whip up any enthusiasm—and all because of Rohan. She did not look forward one little bit to seeing him again, to working with him—or against him—as the case often seemed to be these days.

And on top of that was this new awareness, this subtle change in her feelings, this suspicion that she might be on the verge of falling in love with him, a love so different from what she had felt for Glen that it was frightening. And, more scary still, it felt like a betrayal, as though she was being unfaithful, unfair to Glen and their memories. How was she going to cope with that?

Eventually she dragged herself out of bed, showered and ate a meagre breakfast and then telephoned to see how Douglas was feeling. She dared not risk going up to the house and being driven to the office again by Rohan. She wanted to be free to leave under her own steam.

To her dismay Rohan himself answered. 'I'd like to speak with your father, please,' she said coolly.

'I'm afraid he's indisposed,' came the equally icy answer.

'I see.' She hoped it did not mean he was worse. 'How is he this morning?'

'About the same,' Rohan answered crisply. 'Are you coming to see him?'

'I don't think so, I'm running a bit late,' she invented. 'I'll call in tonight instead. Give him my love.' Rohan's tone had been extremely sharp and she wondered what had put him into such a bad mood. Had things not gone well with Merelda? Had the girl showed her jealous streak? Had he got out of bed the wrong side? Whatever, it did not bode well for the rest of the day.

As usual he was at Courtenay Textiles before her and she was immediately summoned into his office; it was as though he had been listening for her to come. His face was even more thunderous than usual, his brows drawn together, his mouth grim, his eyes glacial. She had definitely not been imagining that there was something wrong. Without any preamble he said, 'What was Jonathan Herald doing at your house last night?'

This was the very last thing Charlotte had expected and she looked at him first of all in total amazement, and then with angry resentment. 'What business is it of yours?'

'Didn't my warning make any difference?' His tone was harsh and abrasive.

'I prefer to be my own judge of character,' she answered sharply.

'And you've judged Jonathan to be a good type after all?' he sneered. 'Your sort, in fact? A healthy bank balance, able to keep you in the manner to which you've become accustomed, and——'

'You're wrong,' Charlotte cut in furiously. 'Money has nothing to do with it. He's friendly and good fun, so why shouldn't I see him?' And what right had he to pry into her private life?

'Was he the reason you rushed away from here yesterday?' he asked, eyes probing and intent, voice deliberately sardonic. 'Did you spend the night in his arms? Is he a good lover, Charlotte? Does he——?'

Again she interrupted him. 'You're despicable. Jonathan did not stay. I've had no man in my house since Glen and I don't intend to.'

'So what was he doing there?'

Charlotte eyed him resentfully. 'As a matter of fact he came to ask me out.'

He gave a bark of mirthless laughter. 'It's a funny time to come calling.'

'He was passing.'

'And you believed him?' Rohan snorted. 'You shouldn't have opened the door at that time of night—to anyone.'

'For your information he was already waiting when I got home,' she told him.

Rohan banged the desk angrily with his fist, making Charlotte jump. 'I knew I shouldn't have let you go alone. If I'd been there I'd have soon got rid of him. If you haven't succumbed to his wiles yet, you're lucky, but I'm warning you, Charlotte, he's after only one thing.'

'Yes, a wife.' She eyed him coolly as she spoke. 'I'm well aware of that. And you have no need to be concerned about me; I'm well able to take care of Jonathan if he steps out of line.'

He eyed her sceptically. 'Something tells me,' he said with cold derision, 'that you're more interested in him than you're admitting, otherwise you wouldn't have invited him into your house.'

Charlotte shook her head angrily, her blue eyes blazing. 'This is a futile conversation. I resent your intrusion and have no wish to discuss the matter further.' She paused a moment, eyeing him furiously, then added, 'There is one thing I would like to know, however; how did you know Jonathan came to see me?'

'I saw his car,' Rohan answered easily.

'So you were outside my house too?' she accused. 'What were you doing there?' She did not like the thought of Rohan spying on her.

'I took a stroll after Merelda left,' he informed her. I was in desperate need of some fresh air after spending so many hours indoors. You can imagine my surprise when I saw Jonathan's car.'

'How did you know it was his?' she asked, chin high, eyes still bright. This man was unbelievable.

'Because I saw him leave in it on the night of my father's party.'

'And you put the worst possible interpretation on his calling to see me yesterday?' she asked caustically.

'Everyone knows what Jonathan's like.'

'As a matter of fact he was a perfect gentleman,' Charlotte told him, feeling a need to protect what little was left of her reputation.

'He didn't attempt to kiss you?'

'No.'

'He didn't try to get you into bed?'

'No,' she insisted. 'You keep saying how forward he is, but I experienced none of it.' Except that Jonathan had declared he loved her! Perhaps this was his usual approach and most girls were flattered by it? Whatever, it had got him nowhere with her. He had also hinted that he would like to take her back to America with him—or had that been in her mind?

'And are you going out with him?'

Charlotte let out a hiss of impatience. 'What if I do? What's it got to do with you? Really, Rohan, you're going too far. I refuse to stand here and take any more of your questions.'

She bounced out of his office and as she made the coffee Charlotte fumed. His insinuations were bad enough, but for him to have spied on her as well was unforgivable. How many other times had he stood outside the house? Maybe when she was in bed? The thought sent a shiver of unease down her spine. She had always felt so safe.

It could be interpreted that Rohan was keeping a brotherly eye on her, but knowing Rohan as she did this was not very likely. More probably he was trying to dig up some further dirt, something else to discredit her.

Only one thing pleased her, and that was that Merelda could not have stayed very long. Why was that? she wondered. Had they argued? Had the girl let her jealousy get the better of her? Had she asked Rohan outright what his feelings for his sister-in-law were? If she had, Charlotte wondered what had been said.

It took all her will-power not to slam his coffee-cup down on his desk and for the rest of the day she could not relax. Again they worked through their lunch-hour, again he gave every indication of working late, but at five o'clock Charlotte had had enough. He could say what he liked—she was going.

He looked at her in surprise when she appeared in his office with her jacket on and her bag slung over her shoulder. He glanced at his watch and a fierce frown creased his brow. 'Where do you think you're going?' he asked coldly.

'Home,' she announced, her chin high, her whole body on the defensive.

Well-marked brows rose, grey eyes glinted dangerously. 'I need you here, Charlotte. We get twice as much work done when the others have gone, when the phone stops ringing; you should know that.'

'Then you stay,' she snapped; 'enough is enough as far as I'm concerned. You're nothing but a slave-driver.'

She slammed the door, unaware that he sat frowning after her for several long seconds. She meant every word. He *was* a slave-driver; he was a workaholic and expected everyone to keep up the pace. If he had been different she would have revelled in it, would never have minded how long they worked, but not when there was tension between them. It was too much.

To her utter dismay when she crossed the car park Jonathan was standing by her car. Her greeting was less than friendly. 'Not you again.'

His smile was wide; he was completely unperturbed. 'I refuse to take no for an answer. I'm taking you out for a meal.'

'Oh, no, you're not,' Charlotte retorted swiftly. 'For one thing it's too early to eat; for another I don't want to go out with you, I want you to keep out of my life—*forever*.' Coming on top of her fraught day with Rohan this was more than she could stand.

He frowned. 'You mean it, don't you, Charlotte?' And for the first time he seemed to be on the verge of accepting that she wanted nothing to do with him.

'I really mean it,' she agreed. It was all her own fault that he was behaving like this. If she hadn't encouraged him at the party none of this would have happened. If she hadn't asked him into her house last night...

'Perhaps if I give you time?' he suggested hopefully.

'No.' She shook her head firmly. 'I'm sorry, Jonathan, I hate hurting your feelings, but I'm simply not interested in you, not in the way you want. Now would you mind? I've had a terrible day; I just want to get home and relax.'

He looked sad but finally gave in. 'I'm sorry, too, Charlotte. You're the girl I've been waiting for all my life.'

She gave a mirthless laugh. 'You make some very rash statements, Jonathan Herald.'

'I mean it. Glen was lucky; one day some other guy's going to be lucky; I'm only sorry it can't be me.' He embraced her briefly and gave her a kiss on the cheek, and then he held her car door while she got in.

As she drove out of the car park he followed, for several miles he followed her, and when it was time for him to turn off to the village where his parents lived he flashed his lights and that, she hoped, was the last she would see of Jonathan.

Charlotte did not even feel like going to see Douglas; he would see that she wasn't her normal self and would ask questions, and maybe tackle Rohan, and then Rohan would blame her for bothering his father; so she did not go. She promised herself she would telephone him later instead, when she had cooled down, when she had rested, when she had got her mind back into some semblance of order.

She peeled potatoes, put a lamb chop in the oven, and while they were cooking took a relaxing shower. Still in her dressing-gown she went back downstairs, checked on her dinner, and then sat with her feet up in front of the TV. It was bliss. With her door locked she could forget the world outside; forget Rohan, forget Jonathan, forget all her troubles. And then the doorbell rang.

She groaned and as she padded her way through into the hall Charlotte could see Rohan's impressive outline through the fluted glass. He was moving impatiently from foot to foot and before she could open the door he had his finger on the bell-push again. She could not think why he was here; they surely had nothing to discuss that could not wait until morning.

She swung the door open, her expression unwelcoming. 'Yes?'

Rohan's grey eyes looked her up and down, seeming to see right through her pink chenille robe, through her blue and pink nightie, right through to her naked body beneath. An unaccustomed heat stole over her skin and she unconsciously clutched the neck of her robe more tightly about her throat.

'Isn't it a little early to be ready for bed?' he asked derisively.

Charlotte looked at him with ice in her eyes. 'I wasn't expecting visitors.'

'Or is there another reason you're dressed like that?' he asked, his voice sharp and accusing. 'I think we'd better talk inside, don't you? I should hate you to catch cold.' Before she could stop him he had stepped over the threshold.

Charlotte had no recourse but to step back also and close the door behind him, but she did so with ill grace and her eyes were fierce. 'Say what you've got to say and then get out.'

'How long has Jonathan been gone?' he asked harshly, and his grey eyes had never been so cruel, the thin, darker line around the iris emphasising their flint-like hardness.

The unexpected question made Charlotte frown. 'What are you talking about? Jonathan hasn't been here.' Rohan seemed to have a fixation where this other man was concerned, making up stories to suit himself, doing his utmost to catch her out.

'You expect me to believe that?' His whole expression repudiated every word she said.

'Of course I do,' she snapped; 'I'm not in the habit of telling lies.'

'But he was the reason you left early, wasn't he?' Rohan sneered. 'You obviously made your arrangements last night. The only thing that does surprise me is that he's not still here. He left remarkably quickly; what happened? Did he get what he wanted and then——?'

This time he was not quick enough. The palm of Charlotte's hand struck his cheek sharply and satisfyingly. 'How dare you?' she blazed. 'Jonathan has not been here—and if he had I wouldn't have gone to bed with him. You have a debased mind, Rohan Courtenay.'

Rohan did not even flinch, although his cheek had gone first white and then red, and the imprint of her hand was still clear. His eyes narrowed and Charlotte wondered whether he was about to carry out his threat and hit her back.

She stood tall and glared at him, eyes feverish-bright, her red hair awry, every fibre of her being on the alert.

She could smell her dinner cooking and wondered briefly whether her chop would burn while she was battling with Rohan. As if she hadn't battled enough all day!

He took her totally by surprise when he pulled her against him and fiercely claimed her mouth with his own. It shouldn't have done; it seemed to be his answer for every argument. Nevertheless she was unprepared and his kiss sent instant sensations rippling along her nerves, causing her heartbeats to accelerate, her pulses to gallop, and her whole body to feel profoundly disturbed. This should not be happening; it was all wrong, too soon, too confusing, too shameful.

But although Charlotte knew she ought to resist, ought to fight him once again with every fibre of her being, for some unknown reason she could not. Whether it was her day-long battle that had drained her of all energy, or whether it was because her heart refused to listen to her head, she did not know.

Her attempt to push him away was pitiful; she doubted he even noticed. She accepted his kiss instead of refusing it, responded instead of rejecting, and it was like taking a drug. The sensations created filled her whole being, spread through every nerve, every vein, every tissue; made her head feel light and pushed all sane thoughts out of her mind.

Glen's kisses had never had this startling effect and it felt wrong that she should respond like this. For the first time doubts crept in as to whether she had ever truly loved Glen; whether her feelings for him had been more of fondness because he was always kind and considerate. Not even in the heat of their lovemaking had he ever held her as firmly and strongly as Rohan did now; his lips had never bruised, never insisted—and she had never felt such a complete and utter response.

Rohan's hands moved with incredible, tormenting slowness from the small of her back right the way up her spine, to slide beneath the fullness of her hair, to embrace the shape of her head, to frame her face while he covered it with delicate kisses. Not one inch did he miss: her forehead, her eyelids, her nose—kisses as light as the brush of a butterfly's wing—her cheeks, the curve of her chin, and finally back to her parted lips—her eager lips!

It was an extraordinary sensation and Charlotte could not believe that she was enjoying it. How could she respond? How could she let a man who treated her so badly kiss her in this intimate manner? How could she betray her dead husband so willingly and freely? Rohan had come here accusing her of letting Jonathan make love to her and now he was doing the same thing.

But her muddled thoughts faded as his kiss lengthened, as his tongue sought and pleasured, as his hands stroked and enticed. 'Hell, let's go somewhere more comfortable,' he said gruffly.

Charlotte knew that this would be a good moment to call a halt, to escape this madness, to restore some sort of balance to the situation, but her mind was fogged, she could not think clearly, and she blindly let him lead her into the sitting-room, let him sit her on the settee where he pulled her into the curve of his arms and began kissing her all over again.

It was like a dream, an incredible, beautiful dream where she had no control over what was happening. Even when Rohan pushed her dressing-gown to one side and cupped her breast through the thin fine cotton of her nightdress she made no demur, merely wriggling with pleasure, letting him touch her, letting him mould her curves in the palm of his heated hand, letting him create further, almost unbearable excitement.

And when, with the gentlest of movements, he slid her dressing-gown off her shoulders altogether, and the straps of her nightie too, slowly and carefully revealing the scented fullness of her breasts, she gave a gasp, felt a further *frisson* of sensation, a tightening of her stomach muscles, and her head sank back, her eyes closed, and she gave herself up to the pleasure of the moment. Glen was completely forgotten.

'You're beautiful,' he muttered thickly.

Charlotte remained silent. To speak would wake her from the dream.

'Very, very beautiful.' His long fingers caressed and tortured, his palm taking the full weight of her breast, his thumb stroking, arousing. First one breast and then the other, creating unbelievable, heart-stopping sensations; and when his mouth took the place of his hand Charlotte felt a wild tremor surge through her, feelings such as she had never experienced before, feelings that made every pulse throb until her whole body became sensitised.

He kissed every inch of her breast, going round and round in circles, slowly getting nearer to her aching nipple. She wanted to cry out to him to hurry but was afraid. And when finally he sucked her into his mouth, when finally his teeth gently bit, she gave a tiny mew of pleasure, an involuntary cry, lifting herself against him, clinging, experiencing sensations that threatened her sanity. Never wanting him to stop, wanting more, much more...

CHAPTER SIX

CHARLOTTE could feel Rohan trembling also—and it was an awesome experience. When finally, reluctantly, he lifted his mouth from her breasts, she saw in his eyes such depths of desire that she was suddenly afraid—and totally mortified.

Guilt coloured her cheeks. How could she behave like this? How could she allow anyone, more especially Glen's brother, to get so close to her so soon?

'Is something wrong?' He saw the alarmed expression in her eyes.

Yes, this is wrong, you and I are wrong, she wanted to say, but caught the faint smell of her chop burning and seized on that as an excuse instead. 'My dinner, it's burnt!' she cried, and before he could stop her she flung herself up, pulling her clothes back into place as she ran for the kitchen.

Rohan followed more slowly, standing in the doorway surveying her as she bewailed the sorry remains of her chop. 'I can think of something far more satisfying than dinner.' He came towards her, and the meaning in his eyes was perfectly clear.

Charlotte looked at him coldly. 'I must have been out of my mind.'

His lips curved in a mocking smile. 'Something tells me you couldn't help yourself.'

'Maybe not,' she snapped, 'but at least it's taught me not to let myself get into such a compromising situation again.' Her blue eyes were bright on his, telling him without words that if he once more attempted to touch her she would fight him with every ounce of her strength.

The trouble was he was already close enough to feel the heat of him, to feel his presence in every single pore, to feel the spasms of desire in the pit of her stomach, and to smell the musky, exciting male scent of him.

'Tell me,' she said, lifting her chin and eyeing him scornfully. 'Why do you keep wanting to kiss me when your opinion of me is so low?'

His eyes narrowed. 'There are some things, Charlotte, which happen whether you like someone or not.'

'I don't think so,' she retorted fiercely. 'I think there's more to it than that. I think you're using me; I think you're exacting some sort of revenge, though lord knows why. I think you're using the chemistry between us to hurt me.'

An eyebrow rose mockingly. 'An interesting deduction.'

'I see you're not denying it,' she snapped. 'But I can assure you it won't happen again. I'm not letting you anywhere near.'

He smiled infuriatingly. 'Wouldn't that be cutting off your nose to spite your face? You can't deny that you were getting pleasure out of the experience, and if your burnt dinner hadn't interrupted I think we might have——'

'We would not have done anything,' she interjected sharply, eyes brilliant. 'I intended calling a halt anyway.'

'Really?' He still looked amused. 'If that is the case why did you let things go as far as they did?'

'Because I...'

'Couldn't help yourself,' he finished for her when she paused. 'But perhaps I'm wrong in thinking that it's only me you respond to.' His eyes suddenly narrowed. 'Are you like this with every man you meet—every man who has money, that is? We must never forget that's a prime factor in your reckoning.'

'So we're getting round to that, are we?' Charlotte took a deep breath and eyed him contemptuously. 'Even though you were the one who instigated the kiss it's *me* who's after *you*, is it? I wondered when that would come into the picture. Let me tell you something, dear brother-in-law, you're the last person on earth I'd have anything to do with of my own free will. The sooner you go back to London, the better I will like it.'

'I might not go back.'

His surprise statement made her look at him sharply. 'I beg your pardon?'

'Working for Courtenay Textiles is not the drudge I thought it would be. I have ideas and plans to expand, to diversify, to get a better profit margin.'

'And what would your father say to that?' she asked sharply. 'He deliberately never let it get too big. He liked it to be a small family concern.'

Rohan's eyes gleamed. 'But think, Charlotte, the bigger it gets, the more it will be worth.'

'And that's supposed to make me feel good, is it?' He was unbelievable. 'There's more to life than money.'

His guffaw of laughter filled the room. 'Then it wouldn't worry you if I bought the company off my father altogether?'

'If Douglas agrees, of course it won't worry me,' she answered, except that it would probably mean her father-in-law would lose out. Rohan had never wanted anything to do with Courtenay Textiles. It was wrong of him to change his mind now. It wouldn't be helping Douglas, it would be lining his own pocket. Something he had accused her of doing!

'I can't believe it won't worry you,' he said. 'Are you trying to tell me that, even though you've worked all these years to feather your nest, if it's taken away from you you'll just shrug unconcernedly?'

She eyed him savagely. 'Contrary to what you might think I've never hoped for or wanted anything out of my marriage to Glen. His love for me was enough.' Except that now there were even doubts about that. She still could not accept that he hadn't been happy.

'How about your love for him?' Rohan's tone hardened fractionally.

Charlotte glared. 'There was nothing wrong with that, whatever you might think.'

'It's not what Glen told me.'

She shook her head savagely. 'He couldn't possibly have said I didn't love him.'

'Not in so many words,' Rohan agreed.

'So what did he say?' she asked sharply.

'Many things,' he answered; 'things I do not care to repeat. But all of them connected with money—so how do you expect me to believe that you wanted nothing out of your marriage except his love?'

'You're lying.' Charlotte's voice was loud with shock.

'Are you saying,' he asked with a frown, 'that you could walk away tomorrow with no regrets—financially, I mean?'

'Yes, I am,' she retorted firmly.

There was something very close to admiration in his eyes. 'You're a good liar, Charlotte. You almost have me believing you.'

She shook her head in exasperation, red hair flying, eyes flashing. 'Why won't you ever accept my word?'

'I've seen it all too often,' he answered wearily. 'I was once engaged to a girl I loved very dearly—until I discovered that all she was after was the lifestyle I could give her.'

Charlotte felt surprised by this admission and wondered why Glen had never mentioned it. Unless Rohan had kept his hurt to himself. 'You think I am the same?' she asked crisply.

'I've become a pretty good judge of character.'

'Not on this occasion,' she snapped. 'And I don't believe anything you say about Glen. You're lying because you've got it in for me.' She lifted her chin. 'There is nothing more we have to say. Please get out of here.'

She had forgotten that he found her fiery temper attractive, and when he took a step towards her she backed away in dismay. But there was nowhere to go; Rohan caught her wrists and held them up against the wall, one on either side of her head, and his smile was wolfish as his mouth swooped down towards hers.

There was absolutely no escape and she closed her eyes, as if by so doing she could shut out everything that he did to her. Unfortunately the embers of desire that still lay in her body were rekindled when his lips touched hers, bursting immediately into flame, sending heat coursing like wildfire through her limbs, making it extremely difficult to resist; and yet Charlotte knew that she must; she knew the danger of letting Rohan's kisses get out of hand again.

With strength born of desperation Charlotte managed to twist herself free. She faced him with eyes blazing her outrage. 'I'll say it once more—get out of here.'

Unperturbed by her anger, Rohan lifted his wide shoulders. 'Something tells me that you mean it this time.'

'You bet I mean it. I don't want you ever setting foot inside my house again.'

He smiled, seemed about to say something and then changed his mind, moving out of the kitchen, Charlotte following at a safe distance. It was not until he reached the front door and had it open in his hand that he turned and said, 'Since it was my fault your chops got burnt, the least I can do is buy you dinner. How long will it take you to get ready?'

The audacity of the man! Charlotte shook her head as she looked at him. 'You have a nerve. Any time I spend with you is under sufferance; if you think I'll voluntarily go out with you you're very much mistaken.'

He lifted his shoulders. 'It's your loss, not mine.'

'It's no loss, I assure you,' she muttered fiercely, and when the telephone began to ring she excused herself and closed the door. Through the glass she could see him getting into his car, heard it roar into life, saw it disappearing slowly out of the driveway. Only then did she pick up the receiver. 'Hello?'

'Charlie, I'd just begun to think you weren't in. That inconsiderate son of mine hasn't been working you late again, has he?'

Charlotte smiled. 'Inconsiderate' was too mild a word. 'No, Douglas, he hasn't. I've been home some little time.'

'Then do you know where Rohan is? I rang the office and there was no answer.'

'As a matter of fact,' she told him, 'he's just left here. I imagine he's on his way.'

'He's been with you?'

She could hear the pleasure in Douglas's voice. 'Don't read anything into it,' she said crisply. 'We're still on bad terms.'

He gave a light groan. 'That's a pity. When are you two going to kiss and be friends?'

Charlotte gave a light laugh. 'It would take a miracle. How are you today, Douglas? I'm sorry I haven't been to see you; I was going to phone, but you beat me to it.'

'I'm well on my way to recovery,' he replied. 'A few more days and I'll be fighting fit again. I hope it won't stop you coming to see me, though? I've enjoyed your visits this last couple of days.'

'I'll come,' she told him, though she gave an inward groan at the thought of seeing more of Rohan than was absolutely necessary.

It was a long evening. Charlotte opened a tin of salmon to go with her potatoes and peas but she did not really feel like eating. She could not get out of her mind Rohan's suggestion that money had been an issue between her and Glen. He was totally wrong, he had to be, but would she ever find out the true facts?

And what disgusted her even more was the fact that she had responded to Rohan's kisses, that she had given away the fact that he could so easily arouse her. She had always enjoyed her lovemaking with Glen, had never felt a need for anything more, never realised that there was anything missing, and yet, looking back now, she could see that she had never been completely fulfilled.

Did that mean she *did* love Rohan—simply because she enjoyed his lovemaking? No, no, a thousand times no, she told herself emphatically; there was more to life than sex. It was a pure chemical reaction she felt—that they both felt—and he was taking advantage of it. He was using it against her.

At the office the next day he made no mention of what had happened, but his knowing smile said more than any words, and Charlotte got the feeling that there was more torment to follow.

Unceasing in his efforts to revive the company, he had brought in a whole new computer system and she was busy learning its intricacies when Merelda walked unannounced into her office.

The brunette wore an emerald-green suit with a navy blouse and looked stunning. She glanced hostilely at Charlotte as she headed for Rohan's door. 'This seems to be the only way of getting to see Rohan these days.' It was a dig at Charlotte, a veiled suggestion that he was seeing too much of her.

'I'm afraid he won't see even you without an appointment,' Charlotte informed her. 'He's very busy and I've been given strict instructions to——'

'He'll see me,' interrupted Merelda confidently, and before Charlotte could stop her she opened his door and walked in.

They were closeted together for a long time, Rohan having buzzed through to Charlotte that he was not to be disturbed. The green eye of jealousy took hold of her and she hated herself for it. Rohan was welcome to Merelda, she kept telling herself; they were well-suited, two of a kind, and the girl was obviously in love with him.

When his cousin did finally come out she had a smile of satisfaction on her face and it looked as though her lipstick had been freshly re-applied, her hair combed, and she glanced triumphantly at Charlotte. 'I told you he would see me.'

Charlotte lifted her shoulders. 'You're obviously someone special.'

'I'm glad you realise that. Rohan and I go back a long way.'

'So I understand.'

'Therefore, if you have any ideas yourself where he is concerned, then I suggest you forget them.' The girl's eyes were hard on Charlotte's face. 'Since he's been home this time we've renewed our relationship with a vengeance. It won't be long now before Rohan and I get married. In fact we were talking about it just now.'

Charlotte hid her feelings well. 'I'm pleased for you,' she said.

Merelda walked out of the office with a swing of her hips and a smile on her face.

Her announcement came as a surprise, Charlotte had to admit, and it proved beyond any shadow of doubt that Rohan had been toying with her yesterday, that his kisses meant nothing, and she had probably been far more accurate than she had ever guessed when she'd accused him of trying to hurt her.

When Rohan came out of his office later he made no mention of Merelda's visit, though he eyed Charlotte closely as if expecting her to say something. She chose to remain proudly silent, conscious only of her throbbing head and a sick feeling in the pit of her stomach.

She had been having a lot of headaches lately, but none as bad as this, and when she got home, at the end of what had proved to be one of the most stressful days so far, she took some aspirin and went straight to bed. She was on the verge of dropping off to sleep when the doorbell rang.

Pulling the sheets over her ears, Charlotte tried to ignore the sound. It could only be Rohan—or Jonathan, although he seemed to have taken the hint at long last— and she wanted to speak to neither. But whoever was at the door was persistent and in the end she dragged on her dressing-gown and went downstairs.

When she saw her father-in-law on the doorstep Charlotte gave an inward groan. Of all the times for him to come calling. However, she valiantly hid her misgivings and with a smile invited him in.

'Have I chosen a bad time?' he asked worriedly.

'There's never a bad time for you, Douglas,' she told him. 'It's lovely to see you out again. Would you like a cup of tea or coffee, or something stronger perhaps? I think I still have a bottle of cognac somewhere.'

'Nothing yet, Charlie. Let's go and sit down; I want to talk.'

He sounded serious and Charlotte wondered whether Rohan had said anything about his suspicions. But the look on his face was one of warmth and genuine concern. 'You're not looking well, my dear. Are you ill?'

Charlotte knew it was no good trying to lie, so she grimaced and said, 'I've been getting a lot of headaches lately, and I must confess I often feel exhausted, but I guess that's because I'm working hard. I don't think there's anything seriously wrong.'

'Have you been to see the doctor?'

She shook her head.

'Don't you think you should?'

'I don't know.' It was probably the constant underlying tension between her and Rohan that was making her like this.

'Or perhaps all you need is a holiday?' suggested Douglas. 'You've looked extremely peaky ever since Glen died.'

Charlotte smiled. A holiday away from Rohan! 'That would be lovely,' she said, perfect in fact, the very antidote she needed.

'I have a friend who has a villa in the mountains in Portugal,' he told her. 'It's very peaceful there; you could relax and forget all your worries. Two weeks would breathe new life into you, I'm sure; you'd come back more like the girl you used to be.'

'You're a darling, Douglas, for even thinking about it.' She got up and gave him a hug. She had not even realised that her father-in-law was aware of her lethargy; she had always tried to keep it well-hidden.

After he had gone she could not help thinking how kind and thoughtful he was—nothing at all like Rohan who kept pushing, pushing, pushing, never seeming to think, or even care, that he was asking too much of her in her present state of mind.

She was on her guard the next morning when she took Rohan his first cup of coffee of the day.

'I understand my father has suggested you take a holiday?' His eyes were narrowed on her face, his expression unreadable.

'That's right.' Her chin lifted, eyes defensive.

'For how long?'

'Two weeks.'

'He seems to think you're not feeling well.' A faint frown creased his brow.

'I'm not exactly bubbling over with energy,' she admitted. 'I've not had a holiday in ages; Glen was always too busy. But you wouldn't notice if I was dying on my feet, would you?' she asked caustically. 'All you're interested in is getting the business back into the black.'

His mouth tightened, and a muscle jerked in his jaw. But when he spoke it was with a quietness that she found disconcerting. 'Take as much time off as you like.'

Her eyes widened. 'Is this really Rohan Courtenay speaking?' she asked sceptically. 'The man who insisted I stay to help pull the company back together because *I* was the one who had caused its downfall? Are you really not trying to stop me?' She had lain awake last night thinking about it and had convinced herself that he would put a stumbling-block in her way.

'I'm not completely insensitive, Charlotte.' Her lifted eyebrow suggested that she thought otherwise. 'But there is a lot to get through before you go.'

'I might have guessed,' she muttered. 'I'll need a holiday more than ever before you've finished.'

But to her amazement the following morning he announced that everything had been arranged. 'Here is your ticket; you're leaving tomorrow.'

'Tomorrow?'

'I managed to get a cancelled flight.'

'But your work,' she protested.

'If you'd rather not go...'

'No, no,' she said at once, and decided to leave well alone. He was taking it far better than she'd expected; in fact he was being too generous. It made her suspicious.

She went to see her father-in-law, to thank him again for his kindness. He gave her the key to the villa and the next morning Rohan drove her to Manchester Airport. 'A car will meet you the other end; you have nothing to worry about; all you need do is rest and relax.'

'I'll do that,' she said, still not quite able to understand why he was being so amenable—unless his father had read him the riot act!

Rohan's lips twisted into a crooked smile. 'Maybe I'm not the ogre you think.' He gave her a light kiss on the brow, a far cry from his heated lovemaking of a few nights ago. Nevertheless it still aroused a surge of sensation and Charlotte knew she was doing the right thing in getting away from him for a couple of weeks.

As Rohan had promised a chauffeur-driven car was waiting for her at Lisbon Airport, but the drive to Douglas's friend's villa was far longer than she had anticipated. For the most part she kept her eyes closed, only glancing occasionally at the beautiful countryside. She felt incredibly tired. Perhaps her father-in-law had been more aware of her state of health than she was herself.

Suddenly the driver spoke and pointed ahead and she saw the villa in the distance, looming closer, red-roofed and white-painted, all on its own in a valley between two mountains, completely isolated, no other houses in sight, standing out as clearly as a footprint in fresh snow.

As the car drew up in front of it she could not help but admire its stylish Moorish arches and its terracotta tubs bursting with colour. It was like an oasis—and was absolutely perfect. The complete hideaway. She was not even afraid that it was so far from civilisation. Douglas had assured her that it would be well-stocked with food, and that a woman named Teresa would call in every now and then to make sure she was all right and to bring further supplies. It was the very retreat she needed to restore both her body and mind.

She tipped the driver, fished the key out of her handbag and unlocked the heavy wooden door, pushing it wide. Inside all was shady and cool. She opened shutters and let in the sunlight and saw a white-painted room with straw-coloured easy-chairs, pine furniture, a profusion of green plants and water-colours on the walls. She had expected heavy wooden furniture and a much more oppressive feeling. This was lovely and light and airy and she smiled to herself, saying aloud, 'This is nice. I'm going to like it here; I really am.'

She found the kitchen, which was another pleasant room with white cupboards and worktops and a green and white tiled floor—and enough food to last her a month!—and up an open flight of stairs were two bedrooms side by side, each with its own bathroom. She chose the nearest one, flinging open the shutters and discovering a room that was as delightful as the one downstairs, with a balcony that gave her stunning views along the length of the valley. The next room had its own balcony too and she could think of nothing more heavenly than sitting out here when it was dark and a full moon was shining. It would be like being in another world.

She stood for a moment drinking it all in, listening to the silence interrupted only by bird-song, inhaling the sweet, musky scent of the flowers below. Far away to the north she could see snow still on the mountains but here in the valley it was sheltered and warm.

After unpacking she made herself something to eat and sat outside in the drugging sunshine. Used to her own company for the last six months, she found it no hardship having no one to talk to.

That night she slept like a log and for the next two days she did nothing but lap up the sun. Her headaches faded and she began to feel more like her normal self. When, on the third day, she heard a car outside she was no more than mildly interested. There was only one person it could be and that was Teresa come to check that she hadn't run out of supplies.

But the footsteps that approached were not a woman's, and the deep voice that greeted her was uncomfortably familiar.

CHAPTER SEVEN

CHARLOTTE jumped up from her sun-lounger and glared at Rohan as he walked smilingly towards her. He wore a pair of lightweight beige trousers and a white shirt and looked as fresh as if he had just come out of the shower. 'What the hell are you doing here?' she asked angrily.

Eyebrows rose. 'Now there's a welcome.'

And then a sudden thought struck her. 'It's not your father, is it? There's nothing wrong?' The villa was without a telephone; it was as cut off from civilisation as you were ever likely to get.

'No, not my father,' he answered equably.

'Then what?' she snapped.

He lifted wide shoulders. 'I thought you might be in need of some company.'

Charlotte eyed him coldly as she picked up a towel and covered her brief blue bikini sarong-style, not liking the way his eyes were raking her body. She had a sneaking suspicion that he had planned all along to follow her here, that that was the reason he had been so nice about the whole thing. She ought to have guessed, she ought to have known, she ought to have been prepared. 'I was actually enjoying being on my own.'

'It's a peaceful place, isn't it?'

'It was until you turned up,' she retorted acidly.

His lips pursed. 'It's a pity you feel like that.'

'How do you expect me to feel?' she blazed, although if the truth were to be admitted she felt a sudden catastrophic surge of her senses, a wild elation that should have no part in her life.

'A little bit pleased.'

'Why, when we're enemies?'

'It need not be.'

'You mean you thought you'd come out here and take advantage of the chemistry that exists between us?' Her blue eyes were brilliant on his. 'You thought that I'd be seduced by the beauty of the mountains and the warmth of the sun and give myself freely to you?'

He controlled a smile. 'It's a tempting thought, I have to admit, but actually I'm here as much on business as pleasure.'

Charlotte frowned swiftly and disbelievingly. 'What sort of business?'

'There's a company here in Portugal who, according to my father, have more than once expressed an interest in merging with Courtenay Textiles. It could be good for both companies. I plan to go and see them.'

'And then you're going straight back home?' she asked hopefully.

His smile was lazy and amused. 'All in good time, Charlotte, all in good time.'

'Where are you staying?' she asked.

'Why, here, of course,' he replied, his tone completely matter-of-fact.

It was the answer she had both dreaded and expected. 'What if I don't want you?' Her chin was high, her eyes still bright.

'I'm afraid you have no choice.'

'You mean you're going to foist yourself on me?' Her mind searched frantically for a good sound reason why he could not stay.

'I mean, my dear Charlotte——' he was really enjoying himself now '—that this is actually *my* villa. You are my guest, and so there is nothing at all you can do about it.'

Charlotte's mouth fell open; this was the last thing she had expected. Her heartbeats grew confused, her legs felt as though they were going to buckle beneath her, and she groped behind for something to sit on.

Rohan pulled out a chair from the white-painted table. 'I'm sorry if it's come as such a shock.'

'Sorry, be damned!' she cried, sitting thankfully. 'It was a set-up, wasn't it? Douglas was in on this too. He made up the story about it belonging to a friend.' She hated the fact that she had been duped by her father-in-law whom she loved and had, until this moment, trusted implicitly.

Rohan hooked another chair forward and sat down himself, facing her, knees almost touching. 'Would you have come if you had known it was mine?'

'Most definitely not,' she claimed, and wished he were not sitting so close. No matter how angry she was, no matter what harsh thoughts were catapulting through her mind, she could not deny that her body was reacting with dangerous treachery. The growing love that she felt for Rohan—and tried her hardest to deny—had not diminished at all.

'Just as I thought,' he said. 'But you haven't been looking well lately and, as I said to my father, it was time you had a holiday.'

'*You* said?' queried Charlotte sharply.

'You find that surprising?'

'I most certainly do,' she replied. 'You spend ten or eleven hours a day at the office, you bark and bite and expect everyone to do your bidding. I didn't think you had time to notice things like that.'

A smile touched his lips. 'You'd be surprised how much I notice, Charlotte, especially where you're concerned.' His voice grew deeper as he said her name.

Take 4 Love on Call

Mills & Boon Love on Call romances capture all the excitement and emotion of a busy medical world... A world, however, where love and romance are never far away.

We will send you four LOVE ON CALL ROMANCES absolutely FREE plus a cuddly teddy bear and a mystery gift, as your introduction to this superb series.

At the same time we'll reserve a subscription for you to our Reader Service.

Every month you could receive the four latest Love on Call romances delivered direct to your door postage and packing FREE, plus a free Newsletter packed with competitions, author news and much more.

And remember there's no obligation, you may cancel or suspend your subscription at any time. So you've nothing to lose and a world of romance to gain!

FILL IN THE FREE BOOKS COUPON OVERLEAF

Your Free Gifts!

Return this card, and we'll send you a lovely little soft brown bear together with a mystery gift... So don't delay!

NO STAMP NEEDED

Mills & Boon Reader Service
FREEPOST
P.O. Box 236
Croydon
CR9 9EL

SEND NO MONEY NOW

FREE BOOKS COUPON

YES Please send me four FREE Love on Call romances together with my teddy bear and mystery gift. Please also reserve a special Reader Service subscription for me. If I decide to subscribe, I will receive four brand new books for just £7.20 each month, postage and packing free. If however, I decide not to subscribe, I shall write to you within 10 days. The free books and gifts will be mine to keep in anycase. I understand that I am under no obligation - I may cancel or suspend my subscription at any time simply by writing to you. I am over 18 years of age.

EXTRA BONUS

We all love mysteries, so as well as the FREE books and Teddy, here's an intriguing gift especially for you. No clues - send off today!

9A4D

Ms/Mrs/Miss/Mr _____

Address _____

_____

Postcode _____   Signature _____

One per household. Offer expires 31st March 1995. The right is reserved to refuse an application and change the terms of this offer. Offer not available for current subscribers to Love on Call. Offer valid in UK and Eire only. Readers overseas please send for details. Southern Africa write to IBS Private Bag, Randburg 2125. You may be mailed with offers from other reputable companies as a result of this application if you would prefer not to share in this opportunity please tick box ☐

MPS MAILING PREFERENCE SERVICE

She stifled a sudden tremor. 'How about Merelda? What did she have to say about you coming out here?'

'Merelda? Hmm.' Both brows rose this time. 'Now what makes you think it's any business of my cousin's what I do? If I didn't know you better, Charlotte, I'd say you were jealous.'

'Jealous!' she exclaimed. 'Heavens above, Merelda's welcome to you.'

He smiled thoughtfully and did not pursue the conversation. 'I'll get my things in and then I can share some of this glorious sunshine.' He sprang to his feet and walked over to the car.

It was not until Rohan had disappeared indoors that Charlotte relaxed and took several deep breaths, trying, without much success, to control her shattered emotions. He was unbelievable, turning up like this. There would be no peace now until he had gone, and how long that would be was anyone's guess. She felt sure that declaring he was here to do business was all an excuse. Nothing had been mentioned before she came out of a business deal with Portugal.

This villa was actually very romantic: a beautiful secret place, a perfect hideaway for lovers. Is this what Rohan had in mind? Did he expect them to become lovers? It would be difficult fending him off when her feelings were so strong. She had tried to deny them, for her own peace of mind, but now he was here how was she going to cope without giving herself away?

She was convinced that Rohan was playing some game, that this was all part and parcel of his plot to seek revenge for what he thought she had done to Glen. He had no real feelings for her, no warm emotions such as were feeding her own body; he did not really care that she was looking tired and was well below par; his concern had all been a ruse to get his father to play along.

When Rohan came out to join her she kept her eyes closed and pretended to be asleep. She heard him drag a second lounger across the terrace, heard the rustle as he lay down, and could sense his eyes on her.

'So what do you think of my villa?'

Reluctantly Charlotte looked at him and was shocked to see that he was lying less than an arm's length away. His deep-set grey eyes were intent upon hers and he wore nothing but a pair of black beach shorts. She swallowed hard at the sight of his hard body, so different from Glen's—why did she insist on comparing these two brothers?—so broad and deeply tanned, a scattering of hairs glinting in the sun, power packed in every muscle.

'It's a perfect spot to relax,' she admitted; 'at least it was until you turned up.'

'There's no reason why you shouldn't continue to enjoy it.' His eyes were narrowed in the sun and it was difficult to read his expression.

Did he really think that she would—with him here? Lord, he was an insensitive brute. She felt a need to change the conversation. 'Does it lie empty when you're not using it yourself?'

'Heavens, no,' he answered. 'It's used as a holiday home, though it's a bit too isolated for most people's taste. It's generally only used in emergencies, such as if someone's double booked, although there are people who come here regularly every year.'

'Do you come often yourself?'

'Two or three times a year,' he told her, and Charlotte was surprised he took so much time off from his work. Was it the beauty of the place that pulled him? Or were there other attractions? This woman, Teresa, for instance, who had stocked the villa so admirably. Was she a personal friend of Rohan's? Charlotte hated herself for feeling jealous but she could not help it. If only

Rohan could love her the same as she was learning to love him!

They lay there for over half an hour, talking desultorily, and all the time Charlotte felt her body responding to Rohan's until in the end she could stand it no longer. She jumped to her feet. 'I'm going for a walk.'

'I'll come with you,' said Rohan at once.

But Charlotte shook her head. 'I'd really like to be alone.'

'Is something wrong?'

She let out her breath on an impatient hiss, shaking her head. How could he be so insensitive? 'This is wrong; you and me here, together, no escape. I don't want it, Rohan. I need time to myself; that's why I came.'

'I'm sorry you feel like that.' He had risen and was standing next to her and Charlotte could feel the warmth of his body and a fresh surge of sensations flooded through her.

'Are you?' she asked crisply. 'Something tells me that you had an ulterior motive in coming here; that it wasn't business, or a desire to be friendly, or to make sure I was all right. It's something far more devious than that, isn't it?'

'Would you believe me if I said I missed you?'

'Like hell I would,' she scorned, even though her heart did miss a beat. 'The only reason you could have possibly missed me is if there was something you wanted to know about the business.'

'Charlotte.' He put his hands on her arms but she wrenched herself free.

'Let's get one thing quite clear here and now,' she said fiercely. 'I don't want you touching me while you're here. No advances, no kisses, nothing.' She wondered if he could hear her rapidly beating heart, whether he knew how hard it was for her to say these words.

'That's a very unfair request, Charlotte. You're an attractive woman; it will be difficult to——'

'If you came here thinking you could have an affair you're mistaken,' she cut in angrily. 'And now you know how I feel I think it would be a good idea if you turned right around and went away again. In fact when I come back from my walk I'd like to find you gone.' She ran into the house and pulled a dress on over her bikini, slid her feet into a pair of sandals and left the house. Rohan stood and watched but made no attempt to follow, and for this she was grateful.

It was blissfully cool beneath the pine trees and Charlotte walked much further than she had on any other day when she'd ventured into the forest, her thoughts chaotic, her whole body in turmoil. It was going to be hell with Rohan here; there was not going to be a moment's peace. It would be fight, fight, fight all the way. He would not keep his distance, even though she had made her feelings clear.

A good forty minutes later she found a trickling mountain stream and stopped to bathe her hot and aching feet, observing a noisy flock of azure-winged magpies, catching a glimpse of a golden eagle, and finally, reluctantly, turning to head her way back to the villa—and Rohan!

To her dismay, after a few minutes' walking, Charlotte discovered that she was hopelessly lost; and when she passed the same clump of bushes for the second time she knew that she was walking round in circles.

What an idiot she was. She had been so engrossed in her thoughts that she hadn't taken note of the direction she was walking. What to do now? Shout? Call out for Rohan? Hope that sound would travel and he would hear her? If he didn't no one else would. They were literally miles from civilisation, and she did not fancy sleeping under the stars. Who knew what sort of wild animals lurked in these woods?

On the other hand she did not want to make a fool of herself; she would try yet again to find her way back. When her foot slipped off a boulder at the side of the stream Charlotte knew she had to be more careful; breaking a limb was the last thing she wanted.

In the end sheer exhaustion made her sit down, and she realised the futility of going on. She could be getting further and further away from the villa instead of nearer. It was still daylight, still time for Rohan to find her—*if* he had even realised she was missing! He probably hadn't even begun to worry yet. She had been in such a mood that he wouldn't fret if she didn't turn up for hours. He might even have fallen asleep on the sun-lounger. The thought did not help.

She began to shout, calling his name at the top of her voice. It was a futile attempt, she realised, when a quarter of an hour passed and she got no response.

It occurred to her that the sun had been shining directly down the valley towards the villa when she set off, so, if she kept it behind her now, she could not fail to find her way back—except that it had now moved behind the mountain.

Nevertheless she could still see its general direction and she set off again with more confidence and determination. Why hadn't she thought of this before? In her hurry, however, she caught her foot in a hole in the ground, felt a pain shoot through her ankle, and as she fell to the ground all the breath was knocked out of her body.

She cursed herself anew for her stupidity and lay there for a few moments until her breathing returned to normal. She got up slowly and experimentally, wincing as she put her foot to the ground, realising to her dismay that it was going to be difficult, if not impossible, to make her way back now, even if she could find the way. There was nothing left for her to do except keep on shouting and hope Rohan would hear.

Almost another hour went by, during which she had managed to find herself a branch to use as a crutch, hopping and limping along what looked like a track through the trees, though she was still unsure whether she was heading in the right direction.

Intermittently she called Rohan's name and then suddenly, faintly, she thought she heard an answer. She stood stock still and listened, and there it was, distant but clear: 'Charlotte, Charlotte.'

'Rohan, this way,' she called and the relief was so great that she felt tears spring to her eyes. She kept on calling until he was in sight, and, clinging to her makeshift stick, she beamed a smile of welcome. 'Thank goodness you've found me.'

But Rohan did not smile in response. In fact she had never seen him looking so angry. 'What the hell sort of game are you playing?'

'Game?' she queried. 'I hurt my ankle, Rohan.'

He looked down, as if only just noticing, but there was no sympathy, still a snort of anger. 'You had no right walking so far. Goodness, have you any idea how far this forest stretches? You could have got lost. When you said you were going for a walk I had no idea you intended coming this far or I would never have allowed it.'

'I didn't mean to,' she said, knowing it would be the wrong thing now to tell him that she *had* actually got lost.

'Can you walk?' For the first time, a hint of compassion.

'With the aid of this stick, yes,' she answered, and with her chin high she set off in the direction from which Rohan had come.

But she had taken no more than a few belaboured steps before he snarled, 'This is ridiculous; I'd better carry you.'

But Charlotte could not stand the thought of being held so close to his hard body, of feeling his strong heartbeat, and the warmth that would inevitably flood her limbs. 'It's not necessary,' she protested firmly and loudly; 'just give me your arm.' She sounded breathless but knew he would put it down to the exertion of trying to walk.

And so, difficult step by difficult step, they made it back to the villa, where Rohan insisted on bathing her ankle in cold water before wrapping it firmly with a bandage. 'You're to rest completely for the next couple of days,' he warned.

Which meant there was no possibility of getting rid of him, thought Charlotte with a groan. By her own stupidity she had created an impossible situation. He would, she knew, insist on fetching and carrying for her; there would literally be no escape.

'I'd like to slip into some fresh clothes,' she said. 'Would you mind helping me upstairs?' She hated the thought of yet more physical contact but what choice had she?

Rohan gave a wolfish smile, as though he knew exactly what thoughts were going through her mind. Before she could stop him he had lifted her into his arms, carrying her up the flight of open stairs as easily as if she were a baby. He kicked open the door and put her down on the bed. 'Is there anything else you would like me to do?'

He appeared to have got over his earlier anger and now saw the situation to his own advantage.

'Nothing, thank you,' she said crisply. 'I'll give you a call when I'm ready to come back down.'

She would have dearly loved a shower but was afraid to risk it in case she slipped while balancing on one leg, but she did manage to wash her hair in the hand-basin and when she had finished she hopped outside on to the balcony. If things had been different between her and Rohan this would have been a veritable paradise; if he had loved her as she was beginning to love him it could have been perfect.

Now, when he appeared on the adjoining balcony, she glared at him fiercely. 'Is there to be no privacy in this place?'

'I hadn't realised you were out here,' he said with a quirk of an eyebrow and a touch of humour to his lips.

Charlotte did not believe him.

'You look like a mermaid,' he went on, 'combing your hair like that. If I'd known you wanted your hair washing I would have done it for you. Never be afraid to ask, Charlotte. Would you like me to come over there and brush it?'

'No!' Charlotte's response was instant, her heart panicking at the very thought. 'This balcony is out of bounds, as is my bedroom.' Her tone was sharp. 'I realise I cannot control anywhere else as this is *your* villa, but if you dare set one foot over here I'll——'

'You'll what?' he jeered as she faltered.

'I'll make sure you regret it,' she finished fiercely. The trouble was, if he did dare violate her privacy, he was too big and strong for her to do very much about it. She could only hope that he was gentleman enough to respect her wishes.

'Brave words, my dear Charlotte. I've half a mind to put them to the test.' He walked over to where their two balconies met, where, if he had the nerve, he could leap from one wrought-iron railing to the other.

Their eyes met and Charlotte felt the full impact, felt the sudden thud of her heart. 'You wouldn't dare.'

'Wouldn't I?' He gave another of his wolfish grins. 'Daring me is the wrong thing to do.' In two seconds he was up on the rail, getting his balance before striding the space in between, and then jumping down to join her. 'I'm here, Charlotte; what are you going to do now?'

She felt her heart thundering within her breast and closed her eyes momentarily. All she had on was a thin cotton housecoat and she suddenly realised how vulnerable she was. Finally she looked at him. 'I'm going to rely on you to behave like a gentleman and do as I ask. I don't want you to brush my hair and I don't want you anywhere near me. I'm sure your father didn't expect you to behave like this.'

'My father would like nothing better than for the two of us to become—good friends.'

The way he paused, the way he said 'good friends' made Charlotte wonder whether Douglas wasn't hoping for something more. The thought was alarming. She had never dreamt that he had anything like this in mind when he tried to push them together.

'I don't care what your father wants,' she said bluntly. 'There's no chance of us becoming good friends or anything else.'

He inclined his head to one side and there was amusement in his eyes. 'Anything else? What, I ask myself, do you mean by that?'

'You know very well what I mean,' she retorted crisply. She wished he wouldn't play with her; he was making it so difficult. She could only hope that he never guessed her feelings for him were growing disproportionately fast.

'I find that a great pity considering the amount of time we're going to spend together.'

'You should have thought of that before you decided to come here,' she told him shortly. 'If you're that desperate for a girl then I suggest you go and find one. How about Teresa? I'm sure she'd be only too pleased to oblige.'

His bark of laughter made her look at him frowningly. 'First Merelda and now Teresa. My goodness, Charlotte, your green eye really is showing.'

To hide her embarrassment Charlotte pushed herself to her feet, saying tartly, 'I'd like to get dressed. Would you mind giving me some privacy.' She clung to the back of the chair for support.

'Are you scared of me, Charlotte?'

His surprise question made her turn wide blue eyes on his face. Her heart galloped but she kept her tone level. 'Why should I be?'

He lifted his shoulders. 'There's no reason, but I still get the impression that you are. Or is it perhaps your own feelings that you're afraid of?'

'My feelings?' She managed to raise her brows and look at him coldly. 'Why should I be afraid of not liking you?'

His lips quirked. 'You're not a very good liar, Charlotte.'

'I'm not lying,' she insisted.

'Not strictly, I suppose,' he agreed. 'My opinion of you isn't exactly of the highest order either, but I wasn't talking about those sort of feelings. Mutual attraction is what we have here, don't you agree? Something that neither of us can deny.'

Charlotte's heart thudded. 'You're saying the only reason you came here is because you want an affair?'

'Not exactly,' he admitted. 'I never indulge in casual affairs.'

'Then why did you come?' she snapped.

He appeared to consider her question. 'Maybe it's because I want to find out more about you, dear sister-in-law. Although you were married to my brother for over three years you're still something of an enigma. This holiday will give us a chance really to get to know one another.'

'You mean you're going to delve more deeply into my psyche?' she asked scathingly. 'Find out exactly what it is that makes me a gold-digger?' Her tone was deliberately bitter.

'Something like that,' he acceded.

'You're going to be very disappointed.'

He smiled. 'Am I? Time will tell. I can understand why men are attracted to you, and how easy it is for you to fool them. You're an enchantress, Charlotte, especially with your hair loose like that and no make-up. You look about seventeen and so innocent.' He gave a groan and quite how it happened Charlotte did not know but she found herself captured in his arms.

His mouth claimed hers in a kiss that was gentle and invasive at the same time, assaulting her senses, catapulting her heart into violent action. Her whole body felt as though it was on fire and although her mind ruled that she ought to call a halt her heart dictated otherwise.

And when Rohan's hand slid inside her cotton gown to capture the fullness of her breast Charlotte felt herself sinking deeper and deeper into pleasure so unbearable that she wanted to cry out. Her lips parted as she accepted his ever-tormenting kiss, the blood pounded in her veins, and she did not dare stop to think what might happen next.

CHAPTER EIGHT

ROHAN put Charlotte from him as suddenly as he had captured her, and he looked surprisingly angry with himself. 'You're a dangerous woman, Charlotte McAulay,' he grated through clenched teeth, and before she could make any sort of comment he walked away, crossing the balcony and disappearing through her bedroom. She was left feeling confused and a little bit angry too. Why was he blaming her for his lack of control?

Nevertheless his kiss had aroused feelings that she would rather have left alone. It did not bode well that she was falling in love with a man who despised and mistrusted her, a man who was attracted to her body but not her mind, a man who was seeking revenge, who thought she was only ever interested in people for the state of their bank balance.

She hobbled back to her room and got dressed and somehow made it downstairs. Not for anything would she ask Rohan for help. The atmosphere between them was going to be so highly charged from now on that it would be difficult to hold even a normal conversation.

For their evening meal Rohan grilled fresh sardines over charcoal in an earthenware fire-pot outside in the garden, keeping the coal aglow with a straw fan. The fish was accompanied by a salad of tomatoes and green peppers and plenty of crusty bread, and they washed it down with local red wine. It was simple and delicious and felt like a feast.

Rohan behaved as though nothing had happened, keeping her entertained with amusing anecdotes, refilling her glass whenever it became empty. Beneath his cheerful façade, though, Charlotte sensed that he was not as unaware of her as he would have her believe. She supposed she ought to be grateful that he was acting like this, but it was impossible not to be conscious of Rohan the man, Rohan the sensual male animal who had captured her heart, who was going to make it difficult for her to get a moment's peace.

After supper Rohan announced that it was his turn to take a walk. 'I need to burn off some energy,' he announced, and the sudden smouldering intensity in his eyes told her exactly what sort of energy he was talking about. 'You don't mind? You'll be all right?'

'I'll be fine,' she told him. In fact it would be a relief. She had not expected any remission of her pounding heart until she went to bed.

'I'll be no more than half an hour,' he declared.

'Take as long as you like,' Charlotte replied.

She went to bed long before he came back, climbing the stairs with difficulty, preferring physical pain to the pain of being held against a hard-muscled chest, to the pain of feeling Rohan's warmth and strength, of acknowledging her growing love but knowing none was given in return.

She could not help wondering which room Rohan used when he holidayed here. This one perhaps? Maybe she was unwittingly sleeping in his bed? The thought gave her an extraordinary feeling and she grew quite excited at the prospect of him coming in here by mistake, forgetting for a moment that she was using it—and... She scolded herself for her foolishness.

Almost two hours went by before he did finally return; she heard his footsteps below her window, pausing as though he was looking up, then she heard the outside door of the villa softly open and close, and movements in the kitchen before he came upstairs. Again he paused and she felt her heartbeats accelerate; but he moved on, opening the door next to hers instead.

She strained then to listen to sounds of him getting ready for bed, but none came so she used her imagination instead. Imagined him unbuttoning his shirt and throwing it carelessly across a chair—or would he fold it carefully or even put it on a hanger? She realised how very little she knew about him. She imagined him kicking off his shoes before sliding down the zip on his trousers—she could almost hear the little grating sound that zips made—and the rustle of material as he stepped out of them.

His underpants and socks were disposed of next until he stood completely naked in her mind's eye, his body tanned and well-toned, an arrowing of dark hairs from his chest to his hard, flat stomach. Long, powerful legs. It was exciting to visualise. Even in her imagination, though, she kept her eyes studiously averted from one distinct part of his anatomy, feeling herself grow hot at the very thought of such an invasion of his privacy.

Sleep was still a long time in coming. It was discomfiting and shaming to know that there was a man in the next room who managed to disturb her far more than her own husband ever had. And all that stood between them were two doors without locks!

She was woken by her name being softly spoken, by a hand brushing the hair from her face. At first Charlotte thought she was dreaming until she opened her eyes and saw Rohan standing over her. Instantly she was wide awake and panic set in. He wore a pale blue shirt with jeans which were tight over his thighs and hips and

Charlotte felt a recurrence of her night-time fantasy. 'Get out of here,' she cried.

'I've brought your breakfast.' His voice was amused, almost as though he had seen right into her mind and read her distressed thoughts.

She glanced across at the dressing-table and saw a loaded tray, complete with a red hibiscus in a vase. This was so out of character with the Rohan she knew that Charlotte grew wary. 'Why?'

'You need to rest your ankle.'

Charlotte had forgotten her injured ankle and she grimaced now, guessing she had sounded extremely ungrateful. 'It's very kind of you.'

'It's my pleasure. Here, let me help you sit up.' He plumped the pillows behind her and straightened the quilt, and Charlotte was suffocatingly aware that she was wearing a cream satin nightdress with thin shoe-string straps, and nothing else! Her heart thundered so loudly she felt sure Rohan must hear, and when his fingers touched the bare skin of her arm she gave an involuntary shiver.

Rohan frowned, though he said nothing, and placed the tray on her lap. 'Is there anything else you need?'

'No, thank you,' she said and her voice sounded husky even to her own ears. Oh, lord, she would have to be careful. He must never suspect that she was halfway to falling in love with him. Not that he would believe her; he would think it another ploy on her part. He would assume that he was the next in line, that it was his fortune she was seeking now—because, after all, he was an even bigger fish than Glen!

He seemed to fill the bedroom with his presence, even though the balcony doors were open and a gentle breeze fluttered the muslin curtains, and it was a relief when she was alone. Before attempting to eat her breakfast she had to take several deep breaths to steady her trembling nerves. How, she asked herself over and over again, was she going to cope with the rest of the holiday?

Eventually she drank her orange juice, and although she wasn't really hungry she ate some scrambled egg, nibbled the corner off a slice of toast, and enjoyed a cup of richly aromatic coffee. Breakfast in bed was the last thing she had expected—or wanted—and she could not help being suspicious, could not help wondering whether Rohan had some ulterior motive, despite her ankle—probably because of it! And then she scolded herself for being ungracious. It was her own feelings she needed to worry about.

But, when Rohan returned to take her tray and asked whether he could help her to the bathroom, she began to wonder all over again whether he had something in mind. He was being far too kind and accommodating; it was unlike Rohan. 'No, thanks,' she said coolly; 'I can manage.'

His lips quirked, as though guessing her reason. 'At least give me a call when you're dressed. I don't want you going downstairs by yourself.'

'I might sit on the balcony,' she said, not realising how prim her voice sounded.

'I'd rather have you outside with me.' There was a sudden gruffness to his tone and Charlotte sensed that his feelings were not quite under control either. Last night he had almost got carried away, had needed a walk to calm him down, and now seeing her this morning in her sexy satin nightie had woken his desire all over again. But that was all it was, desire, she was convinced, and for that reason he had to be kept at arm's length.

'Very well, I'll give you a call when I'm ready,' she said reluctantly.

When Charlotte swung her feet to the floor it was to discover that her ankle was even more stiff and painful this morning, and she had great difficulty in getting to the bathroom. After brushing her teeth and washing her face she dressed in a pair of green shorts and a white T-shirt, and almost as though he had been timing her Rohan appeared outside her door the second she opened it.

'I could have managed,' she protested as she was again lifted by a pair of strong arms, held close against a chest that was firm and warm.

'At what cost?'

To her ankle or her mind? she mused, and decided not to answer. 'I don't want to be a nuisance.'

'You should have thought of that before you went chasing around the countryside.' There was a sudden grimness to his tone. 'Don't think I don't know it was because you wanted to get away from me.'

'My whole holiday was to get away from you,' she snapped, and instantly regretted her words. It was wrong to let him know that he disturbed her—in any sort of way. She was supposed to have been grieving for Glen; that was why she was tired and headachy and always on edge, not because of Rohan.

'Is that so?' His eyes were narrowed all of a sudden, and his arms gripped her that little bit tighter. 'I wasn't aware that I was the cause of your—distress.'

'Is it surprising,' she asked fiercely, 'when you constantly accuse me of doing things I haven't done? When you claim the downfall of the business is my fault? When you work me into the ground and have no thought at all for my well-being?'

'Are you trying to say that it's my fault you haven't been looking well?'

Charlotte nodded.

'Not because you didn't manage to get your hands on as much money as you'd hoped; not because you were planning and scheming to——'

'You swine!' Charlotte spat and if she hadn't been held tightly in his arms she would have taken great pleasure in slapping his face.

'I notice you haven't come up with any proof of your—er—innocence. So what am I expected to believe?'

If she explained that she hadn't given Barry up solely because his company had gone under she doubted he would believe her. And Glen somehow, maybe accidentally, had confirmed Rohan's suspicions. There was nothing she could say that would change his mind.

'I'm waiting, Charlotte.' His tone was icy.

'You'll wait forever,' she spat.

'Because there's nothing you can say, is there?' he barked. 'Have you any idea how much you hurt my brother?'

Charlotte struggled to get out of his arms, but he was merciless. They had reached the bottom of the stairs but they still had to cross through the sitting-room and out on to the terrace, and in her present state of mind it looked like miles, as if it would take forever, at least until Rohan had said all he wanted to say.

'I wasn't aware of it,' she replied tightly.

'Of course you wouldn't be, would you?' he sneered. 'You probably coated your requests with love and kisses and sweet talk, and never thought that he would see through you. You thought you had him exactly where you wanted him, didn't you?' He actually shook her then and Charlotte was shocked by the venom in his tone.

'You're wrong, Rohan,' she protested, shaking her head. 'I never asked Glen for money, ever.'

'Don't lie to me, bitch,' he snarled. 'He was desperately unhappy and worried to death that he had done the wrong thing.' His eyes were glacial upon hers and Charlotte felt a shiver of very real fear run through her.

She was at Rohan's mercy now. This was the reason he had turned up—the reason he had suggested she take a holiday in the first place; not because he'd thought she needed one but because he'd wanted to get her somewhere far away from those who knew her so that he could punish her for what he thought she had done to his brother.

'Put me down,' she demanded. 'You don't know what you're talking about.'

'Oh, I do,' he told her, but they were out on the terrace now and he did set her down, supporting her as she sat on the lounger, lifting her injured ankle, making sure she was comfortable.

His solicitude grated in the face of his accusations and Charlotte recoiled away from him. 'I'm all right, thank you,' she snapped.

A muscle jerked in his jaw and he straightened and stood looking silently down at her for several long uneasy seconds. Charlotte waited to hear what else he had to say and was surprised when he disappeared inside the villa.

Nevertheless tension filled every nerve; she lay there as stiff as a board, her fingers curled into fists, tears not very far from the surface. Rohan was wrong; Rohan was seeing things that weren't there. He was making everything up just because of some perverted idea that she was a fortune-hunter; he had to be. He had somehow found out about her and Barry, added two and two together and made five and decided that she was after Glen's money as well. Glen would never, ever have said such damning things about her, she was positive.

The terrace was in shade, but pleasantly warm nevertheless, and when Rohan rejoined her a few minutes later, a pair of white shorts replacing his jeans, his shirt casually unbuttoned ready to take off when the sun reached them, Charlotte found herself as much attracted to him as ever.

She was crazy; she had to be. How could she feel even the faintest emotion? He was a swine, he was a bastard, he was—the sexiest man she had ever met! She picked up a magazine left out here yesterday and pretended to be engrossed in it, but it was impossible to concentrate. Her emotions were on an eternal see-saw, swinging between love and hate, and she knew she was not going to get a moment's peace until he had gone.

An hour passed, probably longer, and neither of them spoke, both busy with their own thoughts. Charlotte cast covert glances in Rohan's direction but always his eyes were closed; he could even have been asleep for all she knew, though probably he was still harbouring unpleasant thoughts.

When he suddenly sat up she was taken by surprise. 'Would you like anything?' he asked. 'A cold drink perhaps? Freshly squeezed orange juice? Lime? Lemon?'

'Nothing, thank you.'

'It's no trouble, I assure you.'

He seemed to be making an effort to be polite, but if he thought he could lay into her one minute and expect her to be friends the next he was mistaken. 'I really don't want anything.'

The sun had crept over the top of the mountain range now, sending its warming rays down the valley and over the terrace—and she hadn't got her sun-cream! With her red hair and fair skin she had to be ever so careful.

Almost as if he had read her thoughts Rohan spoke again. 'Where's your sun-cream? I'll fetch it for you.'

'Upstairs,' she answered reluctantly, 'but it doesn't matter; I'll——'

'Of course it damn well matters,' he growled. 'I don't want you adding sunburn to your list of catastrophes. Where is it exactly?'

'On the dressing-table,' she answered with ill grace; 'either there or in the bathroom.'

When he returned Rohan had the bottle in one hand, her bikini in the other. 'I thought this would be more suitable for sunbathing.' He dropped them down on the lounger beside her.

Charlotte was appalled. 'You had no right going through my drawers.'

'It was open,' he told her, 'and when I saw the bikini nestling among your very beautiful lace underwear—your very *expensive* lace underwear, I might add—I thought you would need it.'

'You swine,' she spat fiercely.

He smiled, though it held not an ounce of sincerity. 'If I've offended your sense of decency I apologise. I'll go indoors while you change—unless you need any help? It can be difficult balancing on one leg.'

'I can manage,' she grated.

'If you're sure?' He seemed to be enjoying her discomfiture.

Charlotte glared. 'Very sure.'

It was actually quite tricky, but she managed, and when Rohan came out again she was lying back down.

'I'm going to make myself a drink,' he said. 'Have you changed your mind? Would you like one?' His eyes, those unusual grey eyes, were raking her body, penetrating and debilitating, seeming to see through the thin covering of material, hiding none of his thoughts, letting her know exactly what he was thinking. Whether he liked her as a person or not seemed not to matter—the attraction was her body.

The fact that she had looked at him the same way last night was different. Rohan had not been there, he had not seen her expression, he had not felt her heated skin, smelled the heat of her desire. Even thinking about him made her pulses thud. 'Please,' she said.

'Orange juice?'

'Yes, thank you.'

'Ice?'

'That would be lovely.'

She sat up when he had gone, hugging her knees, trying to sort her muddled thoughts into some sort of order. How could she possibly entertain such thoughts, such feelings, such emotions, when Rohan was intent on destroying her? Love obviously did not recognise the difference; love saw Rohan in one guise only—and love was her predominant emotion! It was going to be her destroyer.

She looked out at the mimosa and the eucalyptus, at the orange and lemon trees, and the host of other plants that she did not know the names of... at the tubs of brilliant red geraniums and hibiscus nearer at hand, some sort of flowering vine climbing up the posts to their balconies, a riot of colour and smells, but none more disturbing to her senses than Rohan Courtenay himself.

From the kitchen she could hear sounds of an electric juice extractor and could imagine him deftly slicing oranges and pouring the juice over cubes of ice already nestling in the bottom of their glasses. She was ready for a drink, her mouth so dry it was becoming unbearable.

'Here we are.' He came out bearing a tray with two long glasses filled with orange liquid, two straws in each, and a plate of fancy biscuits that looked too nice to eat. He placed it on a table which he hooked with his foot between their two loungers, then he sat down facing her and offered her the plate. 'You hardly touched your breakfast; I thought you'd be hungry.'

'Such concern.' She was unable to hide her sarcasm; nevertheless she took a sugary confection. It was delicious; she took another, and a long drink from her glass through the straws. Rohan never stopped watching her.

'Why aren't you eating?' she asked at length, more to cover her discomfort than anything else.

'Because I ate all my breakfast like a good boy.' His eyes twinkled as he spoke. 'I didn't realise you had a sweet tooth, Charlotte. Something else I've learned about you. By the end of the holiday we should know each other *very* well.'

Charlotte frowned. 'You mean you're staying for the rest of the two weeks? You're not going back when your business is finished?' This was worse than she had feared but not entirely unexpected.

'I actually had no fixed plans when I came,' he told her, 'but it seems like a good idea to stay and keep you company.'

'I don't want your company,' she cried. 'I'm very happy on my own.'

'You need me, Charlotte.'

'Like a boil on the end of my nose.' Her eyes were brilliant and condemning.

'At least until your ankle's better. You may as well make the best of it, Charlotte; I'm staying whether you like it or not.'

'Maybe *I* should go home.' Her eyes were on him still.

'Now you're being ridiculous. Why don't we call a truce?'

Charlotte snorted indelicately. 'That would be impossible. You hate me as much as I hate you. It's a clash of personalities; it always has been. I can't see us ever living together amicably.'

'A clash of personalities?' He repeated the words thoughtfully. 'I don't think that's our problem, Charlotte.'

Her fine brows slid upwards. 'Then you tell me what is.'

'Fatal attraction.'

'I beg your pardon?'

'We're each trying to deny that we feel anything for the other. Separation was forced on us in the beginning, because of Glen, because I loved my brother too much to hurt him, but attraction is at the root of our problems now, Charlotte, and you can't deny it.'

'Oh, yes, I can,' she countered sharply. 'The root of our problem is the accusations you keep throwing at me. That's what hurts, that's what makes me angry.'

'You're denying, then, that there is this strong chemical reaction between us?'

Charlotte shook her head quite violently. 'No, I'm not, I can't, but I can ignore it. If you think that you can take advantage of such feelings, if you think I'll forget all the horrid things you've said and let you make love to me, then you're very much mistaken.' Her eyes flashed and angry colour warmed her cheeks.

'You're beautiful.'

'And you're insane,' she spat.

Their eyes met and held and Charlotte was the first to look away. The trouble was it would be too easy to succumb; already her stomach was churning, her heart beating at twice its normal rate. She took a drink from her glass and tried not to look at him again.

'I wonder how your father is?'

'Changing the subject won't alter things,' he told her with some amusement.

But it would direct her thoughts away from themselves! 'Why haven't you had a telephone installed here?'

she asked. 'Don't you ever worry that something might happen at home and no one could get in touch with you?'

'Word would get to me,' he assured her confidently. 'But apart from the exorbitant cost of installing a phone, even if the company would do it, I wanted somewhere where I'm never interrupted. My life, as you can appreciate, is one round of telephone calls and faxes, dealing with one emergency after another, making decision after decision. This is my escape.'

'Have you ever brought anyone here?'

An eyebrow lifted. 'You mean a girlfriend? Merelda for instance?'

Charlotte lifted her shoulders. 'Anyone.'

'Actually no.' His lips twitched and Charlotte cursed silently for giving herself away. She really would have to be careful.

He finished his orange juice and put his glass down on the table, reaching across and taking her empty glass from her too, his fingers touching hers briefly as he did so. 'You've gone suddenly quiet, Charlotte.'

'I'm just surprised that you can enjoy your own company. I thought you were a people man.'

His twisted smile played havoc with her heart. 'I enjoy being with others, I admit,' he said, 'but there's something to be said for solitude, don't you think? A time to gather one's thoughts, to come to peace with oneself.'

Charlotte looked at him, shaking her head slightly. 'You amaze me. I never thought you were a man like that.'

'What did you think I was like?'

She thought for a moment. 'I suppose a workaholic. From what Glen told me you never stopped working. Your aim was to make money and yet more money.'

'That's right,' he said, 'but unlike you I planned to make my money by hard and honest work.'

'That's unfair,' she cried irately. Trust him to lose no opportunity to take a dig at her.

'Is it?' An eyebrow slid up. 'They say the truth hurts.'

'Truth has nothing to do with it,' she protested; 'it's your ridiculous accusations that hurt.'

'Then prove to me that there's no truth in them.'

'Why should I?' she asked, sitting up straight, sparks of righteous anger shooting from her eyes. 'I shouldn't need to defend myself; you should take my word for it.'

His smile was wry. 'You're forgetting I'm an expert on women. They can lie and have you believing it if you're not careful.'

'And so, because of one bad experience, you trust no one,' she accused. 'That's pretty stupid if you ask me.'

'Oh, I do trust—sometimes,' he said, both brows riding high now, 'but as far as you're concerned, Charlotte, I seem to have come up with irrefutable proof that you're only ever interested in what you can get out of a relationship.'

It was clear he would never change his mind about her; she would always be a gold-digger to him. She turned away and lay down again, eyes closed, shoulders hunched.

'You can't escape that way.'

She did not answer.

'Only an ostrich hides its head in the sand.'

Still she remained silent but she heard him move and she grew tense. Had it been wrong to turn her back on him? She did not know what he was doing, could only sense that he was very near.

'We cannot spend the holiday fighting, Charlotte.' His low voice was close to her ear—too close, and she rolled away but misjudged the width of the lounger and fell humiliatingly over the edge on to the tiled floor of the terrace.

Nothing was hurt except her pride, but she glared at him fiercely nevertheless. 'Damn you,' she cried. 'This is your fault—everything's your fault; why can't you leave me alone?'

'Would that be fair?' he asked, a smile twitching the corners of his mouth. 'How can two people live in such close proximity and ignore each other completely?' He reached out to help her up but she shied away from him.

'We don't *have* to live together. That was your idea and I don't like it one little bit, and the sooner you go, the better it will be.' She managed to stand but found it difficult to look haughty and remote in a bikini; in the end she turned around and hobbled indoors, sinking down on one of the comfortable armchairs with their washable linen covers. To her annoyance Rohan followed.

'Don't you think you're over-reacting?' He stood in the doorway with the sun behind him, throwing his face into shadow but outlining the powerful build of his body.

Charlotte grew hot just looking at him and she suddenly wished he had built a swimming-pool here, somewhere where she could slide into the cooling water and lower her temperature whenever he came near. 'No, I don't think I am,' she answered. 'I think you don't realise how difficult you're being. If you want any sort of harmony between us then you need to rethink the way you're treating me.'

'You're saying I'm not being a gentleman?' He stepped further into the room and Charlotte felt the air thicken.

'I'm saying I don't like the insults you keep handing out,' she thrust bitterly. 'Is that why you came here, so that you could break me altogether?'

He looked startled by her sudden attack, and then he smiled, a slow, wolfish smile that revealed the whiteness of his teeth and sent her pulses racing. 'Nothing is further from the truth.'

'Then why did you come?' It was difficult to keep her tone hard when her foolish body was responding so strongly.

'Because you're really rather extraordinary,' he answered, moving a further step closer; 'because, in some ways, you intrigue me; because I want to find out more about you. But primarily, Charlotte, because there's something much stronger than all of that, something that you know is there too, something which neither of us can deny.'

CHAPTER NINE

ROHAN was so right. Already Charlotte's heart was thundering inside her breast, her throat so tight that it threatened to choke her. 'If you're talking about sexual chemistry,' she said, trying her hardest to sound angry, shocked when her voice came out in a husky whisper, 'then I'll have you know that I don't believe in making love outside marriage.'

An eyebrow quirked. 'Are you saying that you and Barry never——?'

'Never,' she told him strongly.

His mouth twitched. 'So you like to keep a man hungry, is that your secret weapon? Hungry enough to marry you?'

'See, you're at it again,' she blazed. 'You don't even seem to realise what you're doing. Either you stop harassing and accusing me or you take me back to the airport right now and I'll get a flight home.' She jumped to her feet, forgetting her ankle, forgetting everything except her anger and Rohan's despicable treatment of her—until her leg gave way and she was caught by a pair of strong, familiar arms, their two half-naked bodies coming together, stopping her breath, sending tumultuous sensations through every vein, every nerve, every limb.

'I don't think I'd be foolish enough to take you back, Charlotte, when I've only just got here,' he answered softly.

'I don't see any other way out of it,' she muttered, wishing he would let her go, wishing she could breathe again.

'We could settle on that truce.'

But at what cost? she thought.

'I promise to cast no more aspersions on your character.'

It was a big thing, coming from him, and Charlotte knew it would be churlish to object. The thing was, could she trust him? How valid was his word?

'Well, Charlotte?' His finger lifted her chin so that she was forced to look into the greyness of his eyes, and she saw nothing but friendliness, but she was still not convinced.

She heaved a sigh. 'Very well.' It might be a decision she would regret, but at this moment she seemed to have no choice.

His eyes creased at the corners, his mouth smiled, and she felt his body relax. Up until that moment she had not realised how tense he was, knew only that her own body was fighting against his. 'I think we should seal our bargain with a kiss,' he muttered gruffly against her mouth.

'Oh, no,' stated Charlotte, pulling away from him. 'I know where one kiss will lead. If you want a truce then it has to take the form of a platonic friendship. Is that too much to ask?' Lord, she had been right not to trust him; he was a swine.

A corner of his lip curled, an eyebrow rose. 'I am only human, Charlotte, and you are, without a doubt, the most attractive girl——'

'The *only* girl at the moment,' she cut in fiercely, 'but that doesn't make me available. You'd do well to remember that.'

A slow grin spread across his face. 'If it will make you feel any better I promise never to pressure you, never to take things any further than you yourself want.'

Charlotte felt her breathing deepen as her eyes locked into his; he knew very well that her resistance had a habit of dipping to zero if he really set out to charm. He had powers of persuasion that could not be ignored. Even at this very moment the animal attraction that had drawn them together at their first meeting was making itself apparent. Dangerously so. Hot sun, few clothes—it all added up to passions that could get out of hand.

'Charlotte,' his voice dropped to a low, throaty growl, 'there's no need to be afraid. I give you my word.'

For what it's worth, she muttered beneath her breath, saying aloud, 'I suppose I'll have to accept it.'

But when he touched and stroked her cheek with a gentle finger, when his smouldering eyes hypnotised her and she was drawn even more tightly into the circle of his arms, Charlotte knew that words meant nothing and body language everything.

And she was afraid; afraid that she herself would not be able to call a halt if she allowed his kisses, afraid that the love that was growing inside her would burst the restrictions she had placed on it and allow him to violate her body. No, not violate, she told herself, because it would be what she wanted; but it must never happen, because, at the end of the day, Rohan would love and leave her. He was abusing her; this was all part and parcel of some devious plot to hurt her.

She closed her eyes and deliberately stiffened and when Rohan felt her resistance he let her go, but a knowing smile played about his lips, telling Charlotte that he knew what she was doing, that he was confident she would not be able to keep it up.

And then abruptly he said, 'I'm going out. I need to personally introduce myself to Senhor Correia and fix a time for us both to go and see him.'

'Both of us?' asked Charlotte sharply.

'That's right. I need you to take notes.'

'But I'm on holiday. In any case I don't speak Portuguese.'

'It won't be necessary,' he told her. 'Most of them speak some English and I speak the language fluently so I can translate. There is no problem.'

'Except that I don't see any reason why I should work,' she told him flatly. 'I came out here to rest.'

He smiled, as though knowing she would change her mind when the time came. 'We'll discuss it again later. Will you be all right?'

More than all right, thought Charlotte. It would be a relief to be on her own for a few hours. 'I'll be fine,' she assured him.

'I shall be back by lunchtime so all you have to do is put your feet up and get your ankle better. Is there anything you need?'

'I don't think so,' she said.

Within minutes he had changed into a pair of well-pressed trousers and a crisp white shirt and a tie. A jacket was hooked over one finger ready to put on when he got there. He looked every inch the efficient businessman—even the smouldering intensity in his eyes had disappeared—and Charlotte wondered whether his sudden decision to go out had been because of the build-up of tension between them.

Whatever, it was a relief, and when he had gone she sank back into her chair and felt really relaxed for the first time since he had got here. The scent of flowers drifted indoors, she could hear the birds in the trees, and she closed her eyes and tried to imagine what it would be like if she and Rohan weren't at loggerheads.

It would be paradise, perfect in every way. She allowed herself a contented smile, but not for long. She must never, ever lose track of the fact that he was her enemy, that no matter how nice he was being to her now it meant nothing. She must always be wary, always be on her guard.

She grew restless and if it hadn't been for her ankle she would have gone for a walk. As it was she contented herself with hobbling to the kitchen and filling a dish with ice-cream, which she took outside, finding a shady spot round the corner of the house where she sat and slowly savoured it.

It seemed no time at all before Rohan returned. She heard the car and felt the familiar leaping of her senses but she did not move; she heard him go into the villa and call her name, but still she made no attempt to reveal her whereabouts. Then he came outside and called loudly and when Charlotte appeared from the side of the house his face blazed with anger.

'Why the hell didn't you answer? Didn't you hear me come back? Where have you been?'

'Sitting in the shade,' she answered. 'What's the big deal?'

'Because I was worried, damn you,' he snarled. 'I thought something had happened; I thought you'd gone to try and find your own way to Lisbon, despite your ankle. Hell, I don't know what I thought, but you sure gave me a fright.'

Charlotte began to feel warm inside. He sounded as though he was really concerned. Perhaps he was beginning to realise that she wasn't as mercenary as he thought. Perhaps things were looking up. Or perhaps it was because his meeting hadn't gone as well as he'd hoped and he was in a bad mood anyway!

'I'm sorry,' she said; 'there's no need to yell.'

'Did you do it deliberately?'

'What?'

'Hide, of course.'

Charlotte tossed her head in impatience. 'Lord, you hardly gave me time to get up from my chair. What's wrong? What's got into you?'

'Nothing,' he growled.

'Didn't you get the reception you hoped?'

'Senhor Correia wasn't in.'

'So it was a wasted journey?'

'Not altogether, I suppose; I've fixed to see him tomorrow. How's your ankle?'

'If you mean is it well enough to go with you, the answer's no,' she told him firmly.

Rohan frowned. 'Haven't you been resting?'

'Well, yes, but it's not a miracle cure, is it? I'll need a day or two at the very least.'

He looked at her sharply. 'You don't want to come, do you?'

'I don't agree with what you're doing,' she said. 'Douglas always resisted any sort of a merger or take-over.'

'Times are different,' he told her. 'This way we'll reduce the costs on the fabric and be more competitive. It's either that or the company will fold altogether.'

Charlotte had not realised things were that bad. 'Are you sure?'

'Of course I'm damn well sure,' he snarled, 'and you should know it when——' He stopped speaking suddenly.

'You might as well say it,' flung Charlotte. 'You mean when Glen was ill and I, according to you, failed in my duty. Well, I'm sorry, but there's nothing I can do about it now except give the company my all.'

'Which means coming with me on these visits,' he stated firmly. 'You brag you know as much about the business as anyone, so now's your chance to prove it.'

Rohan cooked their lunch and the afternoon was spent sitting around doing nothing very much, listening to music on the radio, reading, talking occasionally, but all the time Charlotte was too conscious of Rohan's presence to be able to relax properly. It was an uneasy truce.

When the sun cooled a little they sat outside again, but the atmosphere was tense, the electricity fairly humming between them, as they both studiously tried to ignore their true feelings.

'I think I'll go to my room,' she declared at length.

'Is the heat too much to handle?'

She knew what he meant, and it wasn't the weather, but she lifted her chin and said, 'I don't know what you're talking about.'

'Oh, I think you do.' And his face was deadly serious. 'Haven't you ever stopped to think why I never came home?'

She lifted her shoulders. 'I thought you were too busy.' And her heart thudded at the thought that it could have been solely because of her. Goodness, it was nearly four years since her engagement party; had he been hungering for her all that time? If he had he had certainly hid it well. She had known there was a certain amount of attraction—on both sides—but had never thought his feelings ran quite so deep.

His eyes darkened. 'Because I wanted you, Charlotte.'

The depth of feeling in his voice made a raw shiver slide down her spine. But wanting and loving were two different things and she had no intention of turning this holiday into a raging, carnal affair.

'If you managed to control your feelings for that length of time then I see no reason why you can't now,' she said distantly.

His mouth twisted wryly. 'There was Glen to think of.'

'And now you're saying there's nothing to stop you?' she asked, and there was alarm in her voice though she did not realise it.

Rohan lifted his shoulders and his smile became a grin. 'Not a thing.'

'Except the fact that I'm a cheap little fortune-hunter,' she said sharply. Perhaps if she reminded him he would change his mind.

But although a muscle jerked in his jaw his expression did not alter. 'That doesn't enter into it.'

Because he wasn't interested in marrying her, only bedding her. Charlotte felt a fierce stab of rage. 'You can say what the hell you like—I'm not changing my mind.' She attempted to get up but Rohan pulled her back down.

He sat on the edge of his lounger so that their knees were touching and he held both her hands and there was no escape. 'Why deny yourself?' he asked softly.

His eyes were narrowed on hers, almost invisible, but she knew that he was looking at her through his thick dark lashes and alarm bells rang in her head. She mustn't do it; it was crazy, futile, unbalanced! 'You already know why,' she retorted.

He heaved an exaggerated sigh. 'Heaven help me, a woman with principles.'

'Not only principles,' she declared. 'I would never let a man I despise make love to me.'

'Maybe I could change your opinion?'

'Not unless you change yours about me,' she said firmly. His mouth tightened. 'I thought we had agreed not to discuss that.'

'Even if we don't it's still there. Do you really think I'd go to bed with a man who thinks the way you do?'

'There are some things over which we have no control.'

Her chin lifted. 'Speak for yourself; I have perfect control.'

Rohan smiled. 'Shall we prove it?'

Charlotte tried to wrench her hands free but to no avail. His smile grew wicked and her heart thumped and she knew that it would be all too easy to give in. Wasn't it what she had wanted for years too?

She was drawn nearer until his face was but a couple of inches from her own. She could see the fine lines radiating from his eyes, one or two hairs in his eyebrows growing longer than the others, every pore in his darkly tanned skin.

His fingers were on her wrist and he said softly, 'I can feel your pulse racing.'

She said nothing.

'Is your heart beating just as quickly?'

Charlotte closed her eyes, then opened them again quickly when his mouth brushed hers. She snapped her head back but he still held her wrists and there was no escape.

'You're too tempting, my beautiful Charlotte.' He leaned forward and touched her lips again with his own, and his gentleness made it all the more exciting. It made her hunger for a deeper physical contact and it took all her will-power not to press her mouth hard against his, not to open her lips and invite a much deeper kiss.

Rohan, on the other hand, seemed content just to abrade her mouth softly, to touch it with the exciting tip of his tongue, to explore its shape, to torment by the very act of holding back.

How long it lasted Charlotte was not sure. It seemed like a very long time, like minutes, hours even, and yet it was probably only seconds, and in the end she could not stop herself parting her lips and allowing her own

WILD INJUSTICE

tongue to touch his, briefly, tantalisingly, and then she realised what she was doing and closed her mouth again.

Finally he stopped kissing and simply sat looking at her instead, and Charlotte's heartbeats increased impossibly, her whole body alive and throbbing, her resistance at a very low ebb.

For long, long moments they looked at each other, eyes burning as the lengthy contact was held. Occasionally he would look down at her mouth and his dangerous thoughts were transparent. Charlotte swallowed painfully, touching her dry lips with the tip of her tongue, aching, pulsing, not wanting to be the first to move.

It was an incredible experience and the longer they sat looking at each other, the more aroused she became. She realised that the darker ring around the grey of his irises had gone even darker, making his eyes look paler by contrast. They were so intense, seeming to look deep into her soul, as if trying to find out exactly what made her into the woman she was, what her thoughts were, her desires, every single thing about her.

This is madness, she told herself, but she still could not move. It felt almost as though he was making love to her and she wondered how that could be. Barry had never had this effect on her, nor had Glen. On the other hand they had never looked at her in this way, never made her feel so aware of her own body.

At length, when her heart was pounding so loud that she felt sure he must hear it, Charlotte spoke. 'Let me go, Rohan,' she said softly.

'I'm not holding you.'

She suddenly realised that his hands were so loose on her wrists that she could have moved any time she liked. The only thing that was binding her to him was the intensity of her feelings, the locking of their eyes and the mutual hunger that had manifested itself so profoundly.

It was an effort to slip her hands out of the noose of his fingers; they felt like lead; in fact her whole body felt oddly heavy, as though it were paralysed, and she hadn't the strength to get to her feet and go into the villa.

She knew that Rohan was aware of her dilemma. Was he too finding it difficult to move? she wondered. Was that why he still sat and looked at her even though he knew she wanted to get up and go away?

In the end he made the first move. Still without speaking, still holding her eyes, he pushed himself to his feet. Charlotte got up too. This feeling of helplessness was awesome, with the knowledge that he could yield such power over her.

'You can go, Charlotte,' he whispered throatily.

She blinked and seemed to come back from another world—a world of feelings and yearnings, a world where desire and hunger and senses were paramount, a world where thoughts alone stimulated and time lost all meaning.

Charlotte was not at all sure that she wanted to go now. She felt bound to Rohan, joined to him with invisible cords, and several more long seconds went by before she finally moved, before she found the strength to limp back into the villa.

She went up to her room and lay down on the bed and still the feelings persisted. His kiss had been a subtle invasion of her mind—and she had reacted exactly as Rohan had known she would.

But for once she did not feel that she was making a foolish mistake; she still felt this extraordinary sensation of being uplifted. It was a clever assault and although she did not resent it, although she felt no anger towards

Rohan, Charlotte knew she would have to be extra careful in future.

She went out on to her balcony and looked over the wrought-iron balustrade, but Rohan was nowhere in sight. She wondered if he was equally unsettled or whether instead he was feeling triumphant, whether he was now confident that he had found a way of getting through to her.

Not knowing whether he was indoors or had gone for a walk, Charlotte decided to stay where she was, settling down into the comfortable reclining chair on the balcony and closing her eyes. She did not sleep, she did not even rest—there was far too much on her mind; and then she heard her name being softly called and when she looked up Rohan was standing watching her.

It was a relief that he was on his own balcony, that there was enough space between them so that she could breathe easily, yet even so she felt a quickening of her pulses and the now familiar surge in the pit of her stomach.

'Would you like to go out for dinner or stay in? I know it's early but I'd like to know so that I can make preparations if you want to eat at home.'

They were matter-of-fact words but not the way he said them. They came from somewhere deep in his throat, telling her that he was still as moved by earlier events as she was. And the way he said 'at home' made it sound as though he was quite happy to be here with her.

But the thought of spending the entire evening with Rohan in the close confines of the villa, in their present heightened state, was disturbing to say the least. It would be far too easy to carry on where they had left off.

'I think I'd like to go out,' she said.

He gave the faintest of smiles, as though well aware of her reason. 'Is your ankle up to it?'

'If we don't have to walk far.' There was a huskiness to her tone too and she hated giving herself away like this. Her eyes were once again locked into Rohan's, as though they were magnetised; a strong, strong magnet from which there was no escape.

'I could always carry you.'

It was a quietly spoken threat and Charlotte felt a pleasurable shiver crawl down her spine. 'I don't think that will be necessary; it's really much better than it was.'

He smiled. 'A pity.'

And she knew his thoughts ran along the same lines as hers. Lord, this was going to be hard. She had never dreamt that he would use such tactics, or that she would be unable to resist. But, she told herself firmly, she would never give in completely. He could use whatever methods he liked—there would come a time when enough was enough.

'Do you still want time to yourself, or could you bear to come downstairs and stop me dying of loneliness?'

Charlotte did not believe he disliked being alone, not after he had told her that he spent frequent holidays here by himself, but in truth she was bored with her own company too and with a sigh and a nod and the thought that she might regret it she agreed to join him.

To her amazement he reached out a game of Scrabble and they spent the next couple of hours laughing and squabbling over words that were so unlikely they couldn't be real, and then Rohan suggested it was time they got ready to go out.

They climbed the wide open staircase together, Charlotte leaning heavily on him, feeling her heartbeats quicken. Not a word had been said out of place while they played their game but she was still too aware of him for her own good.

It was both a relief and an anticlimax when she opened her bedroom door and he opened his, when she went into her room and Rohan went into the next one, and both doors closed at the same time. Quite what she had been expecting Charlotte was not sure, but she leaned a moment against the door and drew in a deep breath, letting it go slowly and raggedly, wondering for the thousandth time how she was going to cope.

Their intense response to each other made sense really. All those years since they first met and were unable to do anything about it; her numbness after Glen's death; Rohan's accusations, and the anger and the fighting—yet still the attraction was there. While they were working it had been relatively easy to keep apart, but now he had turned up here and they were together for every minute of each day for as long as he stayed. Was it any wonder she felt like this?

She took yet another shower and pulled on a pretty blue-green sundress that was made in a soft floaty fabric and felt wonderfully cool and easy to wear. She wore no make-up other than lipstick and mascara, and put on long, dangling earrings made of shell that exactly matched the colour of her dress. She would have liked to wear high heels but had to settle with flat sandals because of her ankle.

She took a final look in the mirror and wondered if this glowing, radiant girl was herself. Her eyes shone brightly and she looked, although she hated to admit it, like a woman in love. It would be disastrous to let Rohan see her like this, she thought, and tried to tame her thoughts, tried to take some of the happiness out of her face, but was not sure that she succeeded.

Quite how it happened Charlotte was not sure but he came out of his room at exactly the same second as she did. He must have been listening for her, she thought, because no way would it have taken him as long to get ready.

He looked savagely stunning in a lightweight pair of beige trousers and an ivory shirt left open at the neck. These pale colours suited him so well that he quite took her breath away. Glen had always looked good in dark suits; if he wore anything light with his pale hair it tended to drain him, but not so Rohan. His clothes were obviously expensive but he wore them with a casual air that belied their cost.

His smile was warm—too warm; it sent her pulses racing before the evening had even started, and he looked at her as though he were observing her for the very first time. A very critical appraisal that took everything in, from the shining health of her hair, over her glowing face, the nakedness of her shoulders, the aching curve of her breasts, right on down to the very tip of her pink-painted toenails.

It was an incredible feeling, almost as if he was making love to her, but he said nothing, merely smiled, a secret smile that said it all, that told her without words that he approved, that she excited him the same as he did her.

He helped her down the stairs and out of the villa to his waiting car, making sure she was sitting comfortably, that her skirt was carefully arranged so that it did not crease, then he closed the door and walked round to his side and got in himself.

The air was electric. 'Where are we going?' She had to say something, anything, she could not sit and suffer in silence.

'To a small restaurant not too far from here,' he told her, smiling. 'It is used almost exclusively by locals, but we'll be made very welcome, I assure you. The food is superb.'

'Do you always eat there?' He had set the car in motion and now turned away from the direction of Lisbon, up further into the mountains instead.

'A lot of the time,' he said. 'Alberto is quite a character.'

As the road climbed Charlotte looked about her, exclaiming in delight when she saw a herd of long-horned goats wandering through the scrub picking at the grass and plants. She thought they were wild until Rohan pointed out the goatherd who tended them.

Further on a couple of cinnamon-coloured birds with black and white barred wings and long curved bills preened their feathers on the road in front of them. 'What are they?' asked Charlotte eagerly as they flew away, their rounded wings making them look almost like huge moths.

'Hoopoes,' Rohan informed her. 'And look, there's a jay.'

He continued to point out anything that he thought would interest her until they approached a settlement of white-walled, red-roofed houses clinging precariously to the mountainside. 'This is it,' he said, slowing down.

It wasn't as far as Charlotte had expected and she looked with interest at the medley of houses, some badly in need of a coat of paint, others bright and cheerful and well looked after, and in the centre of the village was the restaurant.

It was a nondescript-looking place, very rough and ready with checked cloths on the tables and a homely atmosphere. It was already full of locals, bantering and laughing, but they went silent when Charlotte and Rohan walked in.

The second the proprietor saw them a table was found, introductions were made and Alberto, a rotund man in shirt-sleeves and braces, made Charlotte feel very welcome, even though he could not speak a word of English. His eyes were admiring upon her, and he slapped Rohan heartily on the back, saying something that made the two men roar with laughter, and aperitifs were on the house.

'What did he say?' she asked Rohan when the man had gone.

'That I was a lucky so and so. He thinks you are very beautiful and it's about time I settled down.'

Charlotte's cheeks flamed. It was rare for her to blush but somehow, in this place, with Rohan, with this man making such suggestions, she found it easy to do so. 'I hope you told him there's nothing like that between us,' she said shortly.

Rohan laughed. 'But that wouldn't be the truth, would it?' And his voice went low again.

'There is nothing *serious*,' she retorted.

'But you cannot deny that there is *something*.'

She couldn't, so she picked up the drink that had been placed in front of them and took a sip. 'What is this?' she asked with a frown.

An eyebrow quirked. 'Port.'

'But port's red.'

'Or so the English would have you believe. For years they bought only red as an after-dinner drink, but there's a lot to be said for white port. You can get sweet for after the meal, or dry, such as we have now, to be drunk as an aperitif.'

It was served with ice and a twist of lemon and Charlotte had to agree that it was a very different drink.

'Do you like it?'

'Mm, yes,' she said, taking another sip.

'Perhaps while you're here we'll visit one of the Lodges and you can see how port is made. Meanwhile enjoy your evening, Charlotte.' He raised his glass to hers, '*Saúde*!'

'*Saúde*!' she returned.

There was no menu as such. Alberto returned and reeled off everything that was available that evening, giving Rohan no chance to translate. She laughed helplessly. 'You'll have to choose for me, Rohan.'

'Do you trust me?' he asked with one of his wolfish grins.

Charlotte nodded.

And so he gave their order to Alberto and she sat back to enjoy the atmosphere while they waited. Everyone had started talking again, and although a few sidelong glances were cast in their direction it was with friendly curiosity and warm smiles. Charlotte did not feel in the least uncomfortable.

'What do you think of this place?'

Charlotte turned her attention back to Rohan and discovered that he had been watching her as she looked about the room. His eyes were once again devouring her and she felt a *frisson* of sensation which curled like a snake in the pit of her stomach. She had thought she would be safe here, had not expected another assault on her senses.

'It's very different, but I like it.' She managed to make her voice sound normal. 'I thought I'd feel out of place but I don't; everyone's very friendly.'

He nodded. 'That's right, and you always get the best food in these places—and usually too much,' he added with a laugh as Alberto's wife, Maria, approached their table with two large bowls of soup.

She was as plump as her husband and just as jolly, kissing Rohan warmly on each cheek. Again introductions were made, and again Charlotte felt a seal of approval—a good prospective wife for Rohan!

She guessed the couple were entitled to think along these lines because Rohan had never brought an English girl here before. And neither was afraid to show his or her feelings

'*Belo*! *Belo*!' Maria kept repeating, her flashing brown eyes admiring on Charlotte.

'You've scored a hit,' Rohan said when she had gone.

Charlotte said nothing.

The piping-hot fish soup was like no soup Charlotte had ever eaten before. According to Rohan, rice, onions, tomatoes and potatoes had all been added to the stock in which fish had been boiled. It was a meal in itself and she felt sure that she would be unable to do justice to the rest of their dinner.

But she did. They had pork for their main course with green cabbage, which Rohan told her was the main vegetable in Portugal, and she ate every bit. And *crème caramel* for pudding, though it was served up in such a way that it looked nothing like the *crème caramel* Charlotte made at home. It tasted of almonds and honey and was truly delicious.

Together with the wine they had during their meal and the tawny port served afterwards, Charlotte felt truly replete and very slightly drunk. Rohan had kept refilling her glass, though she noticed he took very little himself, and she was glad because the hairpin bends they had to negotiate on their return journey were truly horrific.

And all the time he had watched her, his eyes narrowed and slightly amused, as though he knew exactly the effect he was having on her. Charlotte had grown warmer and warmer and more and more aroused, and now it was time to go home and suddenly she was afraid. She ought not to have touched the wine; she needed to be in control of herself. All this had been leading up to something, she felt quite sure, and she would have no one but herself to blame if she fell into his arms and his bed when they got back to the villa.

CHAPTER TEN

DURING the drive home Charlotte said very little though she thought a lot. She was totally conscious of Rohan beside her, of the electricity that was pouring from one to the other. Occasionally he glanced across and smiled, the sort of smile that jolted her heart, but in the main he concentrated on steering around the tortuous bends.

All too soon they were back and Rohan insisted on supporting her as she limped into the house. He switched on a couple of table lamps and she sat in one of the easy-chairs because it seemed to be what he expected of her, although she would have dearly liked to go straight to bed, or at least to her room where she could breathe more easily.

'Maria and Alberto were really taken with you,' he said, sitting too in a chair opposite where he could watch every expression on her face. 'They especially liked your hair. The colour of fire, Alberto said, and he'd heard that red-haired people had fiery tempers. He wondered whether you did.'

Charlotte looked at him in surprise. 'You never told me that.'

He grinned. 'What would you have said if I did?'

'I'd have been embarrassed.'

'Precisely.'

'And so what did you tell him?'

'That yes, you did have a wicked temper, but that it was part of your attraction.'

Her eyes flashed. 'You had no right; it's only you who makes me mad.'

'And only me who's able to excite you to such an extent that you cannot sit still.'

Charlotte immediately clasped her hands together, crossed her ankles and glared. She had not realised that she had been wriggling in her seat, that she had done it also at the restaurant, but now he had made her aware of it she knew what she was doing. It was all part of the give-away process. She had thought all she had to do was control her expression; she had forgotten about body language.

His lips quirked as he tried to hide a smile. 'Little Miss Prim now.'

'You're hateful,' she protested.

'At least that's a step in the right direction.'

She frowned. 'What do you mean?'

'You used to say you hated me; now I'm merely being hateful. An improvement, wouldn't you say?'

He still looked thoroughly amused and Charlotte did not know whether to be angry or laugh at herself also. In the end she allowed a tiny smile.

'That's better,' he said. 'I enjoyed tonight too. Superb food, good company; what more can a man ask for?'

Some men would demand a lot more, she thought; they thought that paying for a meal allowed them all sorts of licence. But not Rohan; he might want to make love to her but his methods were subtle and he had given his word that he would do nothing that she did not want herself, and she believed him—whether rightly or wrongly only time would tell.

She relaxed again in her seat and opposite her Rohan smiled, a warm, encompassing smile that sent an exciting tingle through every inch of her. 'Alberto seems to do very well,' she said.

His eyes never left hers. 'Indeed he does.'

It was difficult to stop herself from moving. 'Is it that full every night?'

'I believe so.'

'He must make a lot of money.' Her tongue touched her dry lips.

'His prices are reasonable. I don't think he wants to get very rich; he and his wife enjoy what they do. It's like party time every night. And if he's not too busy then he'll sit at the table with you.' All the time he spoke his eyes were still intent upon hers. The conversation might be banal but his thoughts were most definitely not.

Nor were Charlotte's. Rohan was a past master at making a woman feel wanted. Her whole body was a mass of sensation and she crossed and uncrossed her legs, and then realised what she was doing and made another effort to sit still.

He noticed; he noticed every single thing about her, and a tiny, secret smile played at the corners of his mouth as his eyes left her face to dwell on the curve of her breasts. She felt them harden and begin to ache and her throat ached too and her mouth went dry. 'I'd like a drink,' she said, almost without thinking.

'But of course; what is your pleasure?' His grey eyes slowly lifted to her face again.

He knew, damn him! He knew every single thing he was doing to her. 'I'd like some coffee.'

His brows rose. 'Are you sure? Not perhaps another port? I have an excellent vintage one. Or brandy maybe? Or even——'

'No!' cut in Charlotte firmly. 'No more alcohol; I've already had far more than I usually do.'

'Are you drunk, Charlotte?' The wolfish grin was in place.

'Not yet,' she replied, 'but I will be if I have any more. Is that your intention?'

Rohan shook his head. 'Being with an inebriated woman is not my idea of pleasure. I like a woman to know—exactly—what she is doing.' And the way he looked at her, the way he spoke more slowly to add emphasis to his words, confirmed without doubt that he was making a concerted attempt to win her submission.

'Coffee, please,' she said, maintaining eye contact, letting him know also that she knew exactly what he was doing.

'Coming up,' he said resignedly, and pushed himself to his feet. At the door he turned and looked back at her. 'Don't go away.'

It was as if he had read her thoughts. Charlotte had, at that very second, been wondering whether it would be a good idea to go up to bed. He was far too clever for her, too devious, too sure of himself. And yet she could not complain, because he hadn't done anything, nothing physical; it was all a mental process designed to wear her down in the end.

She could hear cups chinking and Rohan humming softly to himself as he worked. He sounded very happy tonight and she guessed it was because everything was going according to plan. She wondered whether he intended to make his move before the end of the evening, or whether he intended to go on for days like this. She gave an inward groan. It was more than a human body could stand. She would end up making advances herself if that happened—and that, of course, was exactly what he wanted!

When he came in with her cup of coffee he had a supremely confident smile on his face. 'Here we are.' He placed the drink on a table at her side. 'One coffee, cream and no sugar. Is that right?'

Charlotte inclined her head. He remembered everything about her. 'Aren't you joining me?'

'Not if you don't mind?'

'Of course not.'

He sat down, relaxing well back into his seat, his hands with their long-fingered, well-manicured nails resting on the arms, his legs outstretched. 'What were you thinking while I was away?' His grey eyes were level on hers.

'About you,' she answered honestly, but not for anything would she disclose her real thoughts.

'By the look on your face you were thinking something nice. I don't feel I had any knives stabbed in my back. Things are looking up.'

Charlotte was appalled that she had given herself away so completely. It had to be in her eyes; there was nothing else that could have told him. 'I was thinking what a pleasurable evening it has been, and how nice you can be—sometimes.'

'It wouldn't be a holiday if we were at odds all the time.'

'Are you saying,' she asked, 'that once we're back in England you'll change? That all the old accusations will rear their ugly heads and become a barrier once again?'

There was a fractional hardening to his face. 'I thought we had agreed not to——'

'We did,' cut in Charlotte, 'but I like to know where I stand.'

A slow smile spread across his handsome face. 'I suggest we take one step at a time, one day at a time. We'll let all our tomorrows take care of themselves.'

Charlotte was not sure what he was suggesting but nevertheless she smiled also, faintly, apprehensively, and she picked up her coffee and took a sip.

'Do you agree?'

What alternative had she? 'I suppose so.'

'You suppose?' Grey eyes were suddenly mocking.

'OK, yes, I agree, one step at a time. But...' Her voice tailed off. How could she put into words what she was thinking? How could she say that she wanted to be assured of more than an affair?

'But what, Charlotte?'

She shook her head. 'Nothing.' If he could read her as accurately as he made out then he would know exactly what was going through her mind.

Again he smiled. 'I think you're tired.'

'I am,' she said, willingly accepting his escape route.

'I think that as soon as you've finished your coffee we should go to bed.'

Panic welled. 'We'! What did he mean by that?'

'Is something wrong?' His lips quirked as he spoke.

'I—I didn't know you were tired as well.'

'Oh, but I am, Charlotte. *Very* tired.'

She did not believe a word he said. Nor could she be sure whether he was deliberately getting her going or whether he did intend joining her. It was a heart-stopping thought.

'Don't you believe me?'

'Yes,' she whispered huskily.

'You seem troubled. Your beautiful blue eyes have suddenly filled with panic.'

She tossed her head. 'You're imagining things.' And she took a further drink of her coffee. 'Why should I be worried?'

He lifted his hands expressively. 'That's what I'm asking you.'

He was playing with her and Charlotte was growing angry, but more with herself for reacting so stupidly than with Rohan. 'It's all in your mind.' She finished her coffee and stood up. 'Goodnight, Rohan; thank you once again for a lovely evening.'

But he did not leave it there. He rose too and when in her haste she forgot her injured ankle and put too much pressure on it, wincing with the pain, he was at her side instantly, his arm supporting her. 'Poor Charlotte,' he murmured, and she felt sure that he was mocking her. He knew that she had been trying to make her escape, that she had grown suddenly afraid of him, afraid of her own feelings. Damn him, he knew far too much.

'I can manage,' she protested fiercely.

'Of course you can,' he said, 'but it will be so much easier if I help.'

'I don't——' about to say that she didn't want his help, Charlotte changed her mind '—want to put you to any trouble,' she finished lamely.

'Dearest Charlotte, it's no trouble, I assure you.' He was exaggeratedly polite, but more than that were the feelings that were pouring through her. His touch had lit a flame that burned so fiercely, she felt sure he must feel the heat.

With his arm about her waist, hers around his shoulders, she hopped up the stairs. Outside her door they stopped but he did not immediately let her go. He turned her to face him and with both arms linked around her waist there was no escape.

She tried not to look at him because she knew how fatal it could be, but irresistibly her eyes were drawn to his and she felt that sinking feeling, felt herself drowning in their depths. Long seconds passed; seconds when her heart pounded and her pulses raced, when every nerve was on red alert and she knew that something major was about to happen.

The anticlimax when it came was almost as bad as the fear. After what seemed like hours looking into each other's eyes he relaxed his hold on her, and instead of kissing her as she had expected he kissed the first two fingers of his hand instead and pressed them to her lips. He smiled slowly and somehow sadly. 'Goodnight, my sweet torment.'

He held her bedroom door open for her and she had no recourse but to go in alone, to stand a moment with her thoughts before changing into her nightie and brushing her teeth, and climbing into bed still alone—the bed she had thought that tonight they might share.

It was amazing how her attitude had changed in such a short space of time, she thought, lying very still and staring at the ceiling. From hating the very sight of Rohan, from wishing there was a lock on her door, to yearning for his company, to hungering for his love-making. It was a complete about-turn and she was not sure how it had happened.

No, that was wrong; she did know. It was because Rohan's attitude towards her had changed. And because the love she had felt growing inside her had manifested itself in all its glory. She loved Rohan unconditionally— no matter how he treated her, no matter what he said. It was a love so deep that she knew it would destroy her if, at the end of the day, he said, Thank you very much, that was nice while it lasted, and now goodbye.

Sleep was evasive and some time in the middle of the night she pushed open the doors to the balcony and went outside. It was surprisingly cool and she went back and fetched a dressing-gown to pull about her shoulders.

They sky was clear and studded with stars, a silver crescent of moon sent out no light at all; everywhere was dusky black and perfectly still and she sat down in the chair and hugged her knees to her chin.

She was not aware that Rohan was on his balcony too until his voice came to her out of the darkness. 'Can't you sleep either?'

Her heart missed a beat. 'I woke and it felt stuffy,' she improvised. She wished that she could see him, but he was tucked into a chair too and there was nothing to disclose his presence except the deep sexiness of his voice.

'Maybe we're both in need of the same thing?'

Maybe they were, thought Charlotte, but it was not going to happen. She felt something approaching panic when she realised how vulnerable she was, how easily he could step from his balcony to hers—from his bed to hers! And would she have the strength to stop him?

He had been subtly seducing her all day, and now the night air did not help. It was too evocative, too sweet, too soft, too still. It invited romance. Somewhere a nightbird called, the scent of a flower drifted, and her love beckoned!

She decided to ignore his question. 'It's a beautiful night.'

'Perhaps we should share it?'

Her heart panicked even more. 'I don't think so.' Even to her own ears her voice sounded nervous and she wished there were something she could say to defuse the situation.

'Scared, Charlotte?'

She could hear his smile. 'Of course not.'

'I'd like to come and join you.'

'No!' There was definite terror now.

'Are you forgetting my promise?' Amusement.

Not to pressure her into anything she didn't want? 'No, I haven't forgotten,' she whispered. But there were her own feelings to consider. Would she be able to keep control of herself?

'Then there's no problem.'

'Except that I'm tired and I'm going back to bed,' she replied with more strength in her voice this time. She pushed herself determinedly to her feet and Rohan rose too, and she could see him now, wearing a pair of dark boxer shorts and nothing else; her pulses went into overdrive, every nerve-end completely attuned to him.

He moved to the edge of his balcony, she moved to hers. He reached out a hand. Charlotte took it. She seemed to have no control over her actions, and just the touch of his fingers set her whole body on fire.

'Goodnight, Rohan,' she said quietly.

His tone was regretful. 'Does it have to be goodnight?'

'If I want to be any good tomorrow,' she told him resolutely, but when she tried to withdraw her hand he held tightly on to it. 'Let me go, Rohan,' she said.

Reluctantly he did so, but it was with even more reluctance that Charlotte forced herself to limp back indoors, to leave Rohan out there, to turn her back on a night of love beneath the stars.

And when she got into bed it was still not to sleep, it was to toss and turn, and when it was time to get up she still hadn't closed her eyes. A rap came on her door.

'I'm awake,' she called, and her stupid heart fluttered, even at this hour in the morning.

'Don't forget where we're going.'

'I haven't. What time is your appointment with Senhor Correia?'

'Half-past ten.'

She glanced at her watch; it was not yet eight. 'OK, I won't be long.'

After her shower she put on a cream linen suit with an emerald silk vest and decided that it looked adequately smart and yet was cool enough to cope with the heat of the day. She took the jacket off again and went downstairs.

Rohan was cooking breakfast but he took a moment to look her over critically and admiringly and all the yearnings of the night were still in his eyes. Nevertheless his voice was perfectly controlled when he said, 'Senhor Correia will be bowled over. You look very beautiful this morning.'

Charlotte had fastened her hair up with a mother-of-pearl slide, something she very rarely did, but she thought it would look more businesslike. 'I'm glad you approve.' Her own voice, by contrast, sounded husky and still unsure. 'Shall I lay the table?'

'Dressed like that you should do nothing,' he told her gruffly, giving away the fact that he was disturbed too. 'How is your ankle this morning? You seem to be walking much better.'

'It still hurts but not much,' she said, glad he was moving to safer topics. 'Where are we eating? Outside?' It was a relief to get away from him, if only for a few minutes. It still felt wrong that she should be feeling like this about Glen's brother, so very, very wrong. She hoped, if Glen was looking down, that he would forgive her, that he would be pleased it was his brother who had stolen her heart and not some stranger he might not approve of.

All in all the morning went better than she had expected. After breakfast they sat a while enjoying the early morning sun before Rohan declared it was time that they leave. She had exclaimed with excitement on the way when she'd discovered that the textile mills here were powered by natural waterfalls, and the roads were bordered with lengths of fabric and skeins of multi-coloured wool stretched out in the sun to dry. It was an amazing sight.

Miguel Correia spoke relatively good English and was very impressed with all that Rohan told him, even though Courtenay Textiles was in the doldrums at the moment. He was even quietly optimistic and asked why Douglas had changed his mind after so many years of saying no.

He was sorry to hear of Glen's death and the subsequent problems they had had, and Charlotte and Rohan left with the understanding that they come to see him again in a few days' time after he had had a chance to discuss the matter with his colleagues. And of course he would want to come over to England to have a look at the plant there.

They stopped for lunch in Fundao and when they got back to the villa Charlotte was stunned to see another car parked outside. 'Teresa?' she asked Rohan.

He shook his head, frowning deeply, equally puzzled. 'This is a hire car; Teresa drives a Jeep. I trust it's not someone expecting to spend a holiday here. I'm usually told in advance, but with my being away perhaps...' He was out of his car and striding towards the villa, Charlotte following as quickly as her ankle would let her.

She could not believe her eyes when she saw who was sitting on the terrace.

CHAPTER ELEVEN

'MERELDA!' Rohan exclaimed. 'What the devil are you doing here?'

The dark-haired girl smiled with sickening sweetness. 'I thought I deserved a holiday too. What a sweet little place you have here. Why have you never told me about it?' She got up from her seat and threw her arms around Rohan, giving him a long and lingering kiss. Then she looked over Rohan's shoulder and there was triumph in her green eyes. 'Oh, hello, Charlotte; I didn't see you there.'

Charlotte inclined her head. 'Merelda.' And her heart felt as though it had fallen into her shoes. She had quite begun to enjoy their newly formed truce and the last thing she wanted was this girl intruding.

'Who told you I was here?' asked Rohan, freeing himself from his cousin's embrace, his brows still drawn together in a frown. 'Who told you about this villa?'

He didn't seem very pleased to see Merelda, and in the light of her disclosure that they were going to get married Charlotte found this a little strange.

'Uncle Douglas, the darling, who else?' cooed Merelda.

'And was it his suggestion that you come too?' Rohan asked, his tone noticeably sharp.

'Good heavens, no,' she trilled, not seeming to notice anything wrong. 'That was my idea. I thought I'd surprise you.'

'You've certainly done that,' he agreed. 'You'd better come in. You must be tired and thirsty after travelling all this way. Have you been waiting long?'

Merelda shrugged. 'Hours, it seems like. Where have you two been?'

'Out on business,' he told her.

The girl's eyes lit up. 'Business?'

'That's right. Didn't my father tell you this was a business trip?'

'No, he didn't.' Merelda looked extraordinarily pleased.

She had obviously been fraught with jealousy when she discovered they were away together, thought Charlotte, as she limped indoors after them, and was now delighted to discover that it wasn't a holiday in the strict sense of the word.

Rohan went into the kitchen to make their drinks, declining Merelda's offer of help, much to the girl's annoyance. 'You sit and talk to Charlotte; I won't be long.'

'You've hurt your ankle,' the girl remarked.

Charlotte nodded.

'How did you do it?'

'I tripped in the forest.'

'Was Rohan with you?'

'Actually, no,' Charlotte said. 'I'd gone out for a walk on my own. We're not living in each other's pockets, if that's what you want to know.'

'Good,' snapped Merelda. 'I'm glad you've not forgotten that he's my man.'

'I'm just wondering whether Rohan knows it too,' said Charlotte, her delicate brows rising in a faint question.

Merelda frowned. 'What is that supposed to mean?'

Charlotte allowed an almost imperceptible smile. 'He's not said anything to me about you two getting married.'

'And why should he when you're no more than a work colleague?' asked the dark-haired girl sharply.

'And also his sister-in-law,' Charlotte reminded her, not liking the girl's derogatory tone.

'Oh, yes, of course; I'd forgotten,' lied Merelda.

The sound of the juice extractor came from the kitchen and Charlotte wondered how Rohan could possibly be in love with his cousin. The girl really was a bitch.

'Uncle Douglas didn't tell me that you two were away on a business trip. I got the impression that it was a holiday. I wasn't even aware that Rohan had any contacts in Portugal.'

'Then there's obviously a lot you don't know about him,' returned Charlotte, unable to keep the bitterness out of her tone.

Rohan rejoined them, bearing a tray with three glasses of freshly squeezed orange juice, mountains of ice tinkling inside them, and a plate of the delicious sugary biscuits that Charlotte liked so much. He looked from one to the other, sensing the animosity. 'Is everything all right?'

'Fine,' announced Merelda, her beautiful smile in place, her white teeth gleaming.

'Good.' He sat down and they all sipped their juice and Merelda nibbled delicately on a biscuit. Charlotte felt uncomfortable, as though waiting for a time-bomb to go off. When it came it was not in the form she expected.

Their drinks finished, Rohan jumped to his feet and to her amazement produced a portable typewriter. 'I'd like you to do those notes,' he said.

'What, now?' she queried. 'Won't they wait?' She had taken down in shorthand everything that was said that morning but she hadn't expected Rohan to want her to type it out immediately.

He was in business mode and frowned with impatience. 'Of course it won't wait. I need everything down in writing before I see Miguel again. Some people have a habit of twisting things around. Not that I'm suggesting he will do that, but I want to be sure.'

And so while Merelda and Rohan sat outside in the sunshine Charlotte typed. She could see them through the window and Rohan looked relaxed and happy and Merelda was sitting too close, whispering in his ear, and Charlotte could only guess that they were words of love.

And because Charlotte was in a bad mood, because she resented sitting working while they were enjoying themselves, she made stupid mistakes and it took her twice as long to do the work as it would normally have done.

She found it difficult to believe that Douglas had told his niece they were here. Hadn't he guessed that Merelda would follow? That she hadn't asked him without a good reason? On the other hand, as Douglas was of the opinion that there was nothing between his son and Merelda, he had probably thought it was general curiosity, and had no idea that she would fly out here and ruin things for them.

Finally the work was done. Charlotte yawned and stretched and would have liked to sunbathe but it was too late. Merelda and Rohan were still outside but the terrace was in shade and they were sitting quietly talking. Rohan had his back to Charlotte but she could see Merelda and the girl's face was animated, and constantly she leaned forward and touched him, brushing her lips to his, emphasising the fact that they were a twosome. It was probably deliberate for Charlotte's benefit, but she noticed that Rohan did not seem to mind. His initial shock had worn off and he was now happy to be with Merelda.

Unable to join them, feeling sick at the very thought of being in their company, she went up to her room and sat out on the balcony. She could hear the murmur of their voices below, though not what was being said, until all became quiet and she wondered what they were doing. She dared not look.

'So this is where you've got to.'

Charlotte glanced up from the magazine that she had been trying in vain to read, to see Rohan standing on his balcony watching her.

'Why didn't you join us? I take it you've finished those notes?'

'Yes, I've finished,' answered Charlotte aggressively.

'So why are you sitting here all alone?' He looked faintly amused.

'I thought you and Merelda might have a lot to talk about.'

'Merelda is a constant source of amazement.'

'You didn't know she was coming?'

'No, indeed.'

'But you don't mind?'

He smiled, leaning his arms on the wrought-iron railing, his eyes intent upon hers. 'The point is, do *you* mind, Charlotte?'

She would have loved to be able to lift her shoulders in a careless shrug and say, Of course not. But that was impossible. 'Yes, I mind,' she said coldly. 'I mind very much. This is supposed to be *my* holiday. First of all you turn up and ruin it, and now Merelda. What the hell am I supposed to do?'

'She won't be staying long.'

'No?' asked Charlotte sharply, disbelievingly.

'I told her it was impossible. I told her there wasn't room and that it wasn't fair on you.'

'I bet that didn't please her?'

'She was—a little put out,' he agreed.

More than a little, Charlotte guessed. And it was ruining his plans too. He might love Merelda, he might be going to marry her one day, but he had come out here with the intention of using the chemistry between them to take his revenge, to try and hurt her in some way as he thought she had hurt Glen—and Merelda was in danger of ruining his carefully laid plans.

'Where is Merelda going to sleep meantime?' she asked fiercely. 'In your bed?'

He smiled at the acid in her voice. 'Actually, yes.'

Charlotte felt as though a dagger had pierced her heart.

'But I won't be in it,' he added, with a quirk to his lips, 'and it's only for tonight. Tomorrow I shall find Merelda a room in a hotel.'

The pain eased, slightly, but her tone was hard as she said, 'And I trust you're going with her?'

His brows rose. 'You sound as though you don't want me here either.'

'I don't,' she snapped. 'I never have; I want to be on my own.'

'I thought we were getting along very well.'

'All things considered, I suppose we were,' she admitted, 'but we both know it was only a temporary truce; it was never a permanent solution. I guess Merelda's done me a favour in a way. Where is she?'

'She's asleep; she was tired after the long journey.'

'In your bed already?' Charlotte did not realise how waspish her voice sounded.

He smiled. 'Outside on the lounger.'

'And then what's happening? Are you taking her out for a meal?' Charlotte lowered her voice just in case Merelda was not asleep, in case she was feigning it and was actually listening to their conversation.

Rohan shook his head. 'You don't really think I'd leave you here alone?'

'I'd prefer it,' she snapped.

'But it's not what I want,' he returned darkly. 'No, I thought we'd eat in, the three of us; I'll do the cooking.'

Charlotte shook her head. 'I'll give it a miss if you don't mind; I'm not really hungry anyway.' She could not bear the thought of sitting watching Merelda fawn all over him.

Rohan's face tightened. 'Don't be ridiculous, Charlotte. I cannot let you shut yourself away while I entertain Merelda.'

'Why not?' she asked. 'She is your girlfriend, after all. You are going to marry her. She has every right to expect your company and not mine.'

His eyes narrowed. 'Is that what you think, that Merelda and I are going to get married?'

'Aren't you?' she asked. 'It's what she told me.'

'Did she now?' He looked thoughtful all of a sudden. 'Merelda and I have discussed marriage, yes,' he agreed, 'but we're not engaged or anything like that, so at this moment in time I do not consider her any more important than I do you. And I want you with me, Charlotte.'

With ill grace she gave in. 'Very well, but don't be surprised if the evening is a disaster. Merelda will be as much against me joining you as I am.'

He shook his head. 'You're imagining things, Charlotte.'

'Am I?' she asked. 'Why else would Merelda come all this way—if it wasn't to make sure I wasn't stealing her boyfriend?'

'Maybe Merelda does have some fixed notion in her mind,' he agreed, 'but——'

'And you're saying that you haven't?' Charlotte cut in fiercely. 'Just because you haven't put a ring on her finger you see yourself as a free man, free to play around with me without a pang of conscience. That's the top and bottom of it, isn't it? And when you've had your fun then you'll go back to your precious Merelda and marry her, and I'll never enter your thoughts again.'

She pushed herself to her feet, ignoring his, 'Charlotte, wait!' and limped back into the bedroom, closing the doors, telling him without words that the conversation was ended and she did not want to speak about it again.

She stayed in her room until she judged it about time to get ready for dinner. She was not looking forward to the occasion. She could not help thinking about Merelda, wondering what the girl was doing now, whether she was still sleeping off the ravages of her journey, whether she was in the kitchen with Rohan, or even in the room next door preparing herself also for the evening that lay ahead.

Charlotte took a shower, made up her face carefully, and after a lot of deliberation over what to wear chose a white shantung shift dress, tying a tan chiffon scarf about her waist and another in her hair bandeau-style. A pair of gold earrings, a gold bracelet on her wrist, a pair of tan sandals, and she was ready. She gave herself one final, critical glance in the mirror, pleased with her appearance, knowing that she would need this armour of glamour and self-control to get through the evening that lay ahead.

It would be difficult not to show her jealousy; it would be heart-wrenching in fact to watch the two of them together, and even at this late stage she wondered whether she could get out of it, whether she could think up some valid excuse to stay in her room. This holiday was proving no holiday at all.

When she went downstairs she could hear their muted voices in the kitchen and as she had no wish to join them Charlotte stood and admired the table that had been set in the dining area. Plain white china on a white cloth and a single white arum lily in a narrow-necked green glass vase. Very simple and yet effective. Green linen napkins completed the setting and the whole blended beautifully with the rest of the room. Rohan, or whoever had helped him kit the house out, had obviously chosen everything with extreme care.

'Would you like an aperitif, Charlotte?' Rohan called out from the kitchen.

Charlotte was not aware that he had heard her come down. The man had to have a sixth sense. 'No, thanks.'

'Then perhaps you would like to take your seat?' He had come up suddenly behind her and his hand touched her arm, triggering off a dangerous reaction, in spite of the fact that Merelda had followed him into the room.

The brunette had changed into a strapless dress of flamboyant reds and yellows and orange; she looked like an exotic hothouse bloom and her smile was supreme as she looked at Charlotte.

Rohan made sure they were both sitting comfortably before he disappeared into the kitchen again and then returned with their starters. He seemed to be quite enjoying the situation, smiling happily from one to the other, not giving either of them his complete attention.

Charlotte had expected something simple like melon; instead he had made pancakes and stuffed them with—she cut into it experimentally—prawns in sauce! Unusual and delicious, she decided as she tasted it.

'You like?' Rohan was watching her.

'Very much,' she agreed. 'You continue to amaze me.'

'Oh, didn't you know,' said Merelda, 'Rohan's an excellent cook? He's a man of many hidden talents, aren't you, darling?' She touched her hand to his arm, her nail-polish matching exactly the red in her dress.

He smiled at her tenderly.

Charlotte felt sick and all of a sudden the pancake lost its flavour.

He filled their glasses with a perfect dry white wine. 'Locally produced, of course,' he told them, and Merelda raised her glass. 'To us.' She meant to herself and Rohan, of course, but managed to make it sound as though Charlotte was included.

'To us,' Charlotte said weakly.

'To us,' repeated Rohan, looking first of all at Charlotte, a long, lingering look, and then at Merelda. The girl was frowning.

For their main course they had quail accompanied by rice, and some sticky concoction for dessert that came, he told them, from a recipe of Maria's.

Charlotte could not help thinking how different the meal would have been if it hadn't been for their unwanted third guest. She had started to feel more comfortable in Rohan's presence, there had been a positive interaction between them, and now Merelda had wrecked the whole thing. On the other hand she had made Charlotte see clearly the danger of becoming too involved. Perhaps the brunette had done her a favour after all?

After their meal Merelda suggested taking their coffee outside, but Charlotte shook her head. 'Not for me, thank you. My ankle's playing up; I think I'll go to my room and rest.'

It was an excuse and Rohan knew it for he frowned harshly. 'Of course you must join us, Charlotte. You can rest equally well outside.'

And so she was compelled to sit on the terrace and listen to Merelda's constant chatter; listen to her relating tales from their youth, some of the escapades they had got up to, anything and everything the dark-haired girl could think of involving Rohan.

Charlotte was well aware that it was designed to make her feel left out but she did not give Merelda the pleasure of knowing how much she was hurt; she listened attentively, coming up with stories of her own, feeling a sense of achievement when Rohan paid her equally as much attention as he did his cousin.

Eventually Charlotte yawned and announced she was going to bed, and Rohan suggested they all did the same. 'You must be tired too, Merelda, after your journey.'

'No, I'm not,' she said blithely, 'I had a sleep earlier, don't forget.'

'Well, I'm tired,' he said. 'I think Charlotte's idea is an excellent one.'

Merelda looked put out that she was not going to get any more time alone with Rohan and she shot Charlotte a venomous look as they entered the villa, and deliberately hung back so that she could give Rohan a goodnight kiss.

Charlotte found it impossible to sleep knowing that Merelda was in Rohan's bed. She tossed and turned, her mind in turmoil, her thoughts flitting this way and that, and when she heard padded footsteps going past her door her worst fears were realised. Merelda was on her way downstairs; Merelda had no intention of sleeping on her own.

Unable to help herself, Charlotte tiptoed out on to the balcony and saw light spilling out on to the terrace from the sitting-room where Rohan had bedded down for the night. Her imagination worked overtime, especially when the light went out, but she did not hear Merelda come back to bed.

WILD INJUSTICE

The next morning they breakfasted on the terrace, Merelda bright and cheerful, looking like a cat who had stolen the cream. Charlotte herself felt tired and jaded and extremely ill-tempered, and Rohan asked her more than once whether she was all right.

It was a relief when he announced that Merelda was departing. 'And I'm going to help her find somewhere to stay,' he told Charlotte. 'I'm not sure how long I'll be.'

'Take forever,' muttered Charlotte under her breath.

She sat outside with her thoughts after they had gone, wondering whether Rohan would ever marry Merelda, or whether it was all wishful thinking on the girl's part. Rohan was not a man to wear his heart on his sleeve and it was difficult to know exactly what his feelings were.

In any case, even if he didn't get married, once he had finished sorting out his father's business he would go back to London and she would never see him again. This truce meant nothing. It was a way of getting through to her! All part and parcel of his devious planning and plotting.

It was only a little after lunch when she heard a car and saw Rohan stepping out of a taxi. He had left his own car here to go with Merelda in hers. Just looking at him made Charlotte's heart thud and her senses go into a spin. 'I didn't expect you back this early,' she said huskily, looking up from her seat on the terrace.

'I was worried about you,' he said. 'You didn't look well at breakfast.'

'I had trouble sleeping, that's all,' she told him, taking a sip from the glass of wine she had poured herself.

'Why?'

'I guess because I was wondering what's going to happen.'

'Between Merelda and me?' he asked, a light gleaming in his eyes.

'Heavens, no!' she exclaimed. 'Your girlfriend's the least of my worries. I was thinking about the merger, wondering whether it really will work.'

He look disappointed that her thoughts had nothing to do with him. 'I have every hope,' he told her.

'And your father—I keep thinking about him as well. I wonder how he is? I wish there were some way we could get in touch.'

'Merelda says he's fine.'

'But that isn't the same, is it?' she asserted. 'I wish I could speak to him.'

'You think a lot of him, don't you?' His hand touched her arm, his fingers drifting lazily along its length, stroking, inciting, causing complete chaos.

Charlotte knew she ought to snatch her arm away but for some reason found herself unable to move. 'He was more like a father to me than my own ever was.'

'You sound as though you really mean that, Charlotte.'

'I do.'

'You make it sound as though it wasn't altogether the money that attracted you to my family.' He looked faintly surprised at his own discovery.

Charlotte was in no mood for arguing, for declaring that she had already told him that a thousand times. She had been thinking about Rohan so much today that now he was here she wanted to enjoy these few minutes they were spending together in case there were not many more of them. She put her hand on top of Rohan's, stilled his stroking, let her fingers feel his hair-roughened skin instead.

He took a sharp breath and suddenly, unexpectedly, she was drawn into the circle of his arms, somehow lifted on to his lap, and she felt the strong unsteady beat of his heart.

'Merelda...' she protested.

'Forget Merelda,' he muttered, cupping her chin and looking long and wonderingly into her eyes. Charlotte moistened her lips with the tip of her tongue and it was as though it was a signal. Rohan groaned and his mouth came slowly towards hers. Their mouths met and held, tongues touched and explored, and Charlotte's excitement grew.

His fingers stroked her breast through the thin silky material of her sun-top and it was as though he were touching her naked skin—better even, because his hand slid so easily over the silk, it was the most incredibly erotic sensation she had ever experienced and she could not stop herself from squirming on his lap.

Her breathing quickened and deepened and her eyes were like glowing coals as she looked into Rohan's intense face. 'We shouldn't be doing this, Rohan. Merelda, she will——'

'Forget Merelda,' he repeated hoarsely. He took her nipple between thumb and forefinger and Charlotte wanted to cry out her pleasure, but some inner instinct made her refrain. It was far too dangerous to let herself get carried away on this tide of passion which meant nothing to him and everything to her. It was a game Rohan was playing. He wanted her to get hurt; that was the top and bottom of it. Merelda had come dangerously close to ruining things for him but now he had got rid of her and was intent on carrying on where he had left off. She began to struggle.

'Charlotte?' A heavy frown drew his brows together.

'It is best,' Charlotte said.

He smiled suddenly, as though he knew what she was thinking. 'For our sanity?' he asked.

'For *my* peace of mind,' she agreed.

Back on her own seat, she took a desperately needed drink, set the glass down, and studiously avoided looking at Rohan.

'It won't go away by avoiding it.'

She looked at him then, sharply and resentfully. 'You're being unfair.'

He grinned. 'I thought all was fair in love and war. Isn't that what they say?'

'We're certainly at war,' she agreed, 'but love?' She raised her brows. 'That would take a miracle.' He would never, ever fall in love with her; she was very sure of that.

'It was purely a figure of speech.'

'Whatever,' she said, 'I still think you're being unfair.'

'Because I arouse you like no other man ever has?'

How did he know no one else had ever managed to make her feel like this? She tilted her chin. 'Such modesty!'

'But I'm right, aren't I? Even my darling brother didn't have it in him to make you feel this good.'

'You have a monumental ego,' she snapped.

'You haven't answered my question.'

'Nor do I intend to,' she riposted.

'Scared?' he mocked.

'Simply being sensible,' she told him.

'Hell, who wants to be sensible in a place like this? It's magical, don't you agree?'

Too magical! But she wasn't going to admit it. 'You're impossible,' she cried instead. 'Whatever would Merelda think if she could see you now?'

'I've told you to forget Merelda.' He sounded really impatient this time.

'That's a bit impossible, isn't it?' she blazed. 'It's obvious she knows what you're like, otherwise she wouldn't have come chasing all the way out here to check up on you. I'm amazed you managed to persuade her to book into a hotel. You must have spun her some mightily fancy story about us.'

He leaned forward and caught her hand. 'Charlotte, you're getting all worked up over nothing.'

'Nothing?' she cried. 'You're harassing me, Rohan; how can that be nothing?'

A frown settled on his brow. 'I wasn't aware that I was; I thought you were enjoying the game too.'

Charlotte closed her eyes, feeling an impossible sadness. So it was a game! He was admitting it at last. A game called revenge. And she didn't want it to be a game; she wanted it to be for real; she loved Rohan—she loved him so much.

'Charlotte?' He looked concernedly into her face.

'How can I enjoy such a game when there's no future between us?' she asked him point-blank.

'Because of Merelda?'

She shook her head. 'Not because of Merelda, she's only part of it, but because of—*me*, the way *I* feel,' she told him tightly. Could anyone be more stupid than to fall in love with a man who was intent only on hurting her?

A mask came surprisingly and suddenly over his face, hiding everything that he thought and felt. He let her go. 'I'm sorry you feel that way, Charlotte. I thought—oh, never mind what I thought.' He sprang to his feet and went indoors and she heard him running up the wooden stairs. His bedroom door slammed behind him.

Charlotte felt like crying.

CHAPTER TWELVE

THE next few days were purgatory. Rohan went out for a few hours each morning and Charlotte presumed he spent them with Merelda. He never said and she never asked. As far as she was concerned he might as well have moved in with Merelda, because he neither touched nor kissed her again, and Charlotte found this far more unsettling than when he had played with her emotions—even more disturbing than when they had argued. At least then she had felt alive and spirited; now she felt at her lowest ebb, possibly even more upset than when Glen had died, and that felt callous, but it was true.

This new love was different, nothing like her feelings for Glen. Perhaps, in one respect, Rohan had been right—she had been more in love with what Glen stood for than the man himself. Not from a mercenary point of view, but because for once in her life she had felt loved and emotionally secure. That security had gone and with it had come problems—the biggest of which was Rohan.

They visited the mill again and things looked promising for the merger. Senhor Correia arranged a meeting in England for just as soon as they got back, and Charlotte tried to forget her differences with Rohan while they were in the man's office.

And then, suddenly, Rohan announced that he was flying back to England. He could not have dealt Charlotte a more crippling blow. 'I am urgently needed at my office,' he said. 'Alberto took the call. I'm sorry to have to leave you.'

'And Merelda—is she going home too?' asked Charlotte crisply.

'As a matter of fact, yes.'

He managed to look guilty and Charlotte knew that he was using work as an excuse, and the next time she saw them they would probably be planning their wedding. She felt as though her world had crumbled, every hope dashed. Merelda had won, Merelda had succeeded in taking him away from her.

'You will be all right?' Rohan asked, and she thought he sounded anxious, but how could that be?

'It will be heaven to be on my own again,' she told him with forced cheerfulness.

His mouth tightened. 'Teresa will bring in more food supplies. If there is anything further you need you only have to ask. And Alberto's daughter, who is about your age, will drop in to see you each day. She passes here on her way to work.'

'I don't need anyone calling to see me,' Charlotte tossed at him angrily. 'I managed perfectly all right before you came; I can manage again.'

'I shall feel happier,' he told her. 'And I'd like you to promise me one thing.'

She looked at him questioningly.

'That you won't go off walking again.'

Her eyes flashed. 'I'll have no reason to want to escape, will I?'

A muscle jerked in his jaw and he seemed about to say something, then he turned and left and the villa felt more empty than she could ever have imagined. Rohan had filled it with his presence; he had been there in every single corner, each way she turned, every breath she took, and now there was nothing.

He had actually succeeded far better than he could have ever hoped. He had won her affection and then destroyed her totally by confessing that it was all a game.

The day was long, the night even more so; Charlotte had never felt so alone and unhappy in her life. Sunbathing was no pleasure without Rohan at her side, without his eyes stirring her feelings, without all the emotions she now associated with him. Meals eaten alone weren't the same. Nothing was the same.

Isabel, Alberto's daughter, duly called in to see her on her way home from work. She was in actual fact much younger than Charlotte—about twenty-two—dark-haired and beautiful with flashing white teeth and an extrovert personality.

'I come to see you all right,' she said cheerfully. 'Rohan, he worry.'

Her face lit up when she said Rohan's name and instantly Charlotte began to wonder whether this girl had been the attraction when he spent his holidays here. She seemed to know her way about the villa, almost heading to the kitchen in front of her when Charlotte suggested a cool drink.

'You and Rohan—you are—er——?' She spread her hands expansively as she searched for the right word.

Charlotte immediately shook her head. 'We are nothing. He is my brother-in-law, you understand? He does not mean anything to me.'

The girl frowned. 'That is not right. I think Rohan, he love you. He tell my *pai*, my—er—father.'

Charlotte looked at Isabel in complete astonishment. 'Are you sure?'

'*Sim*—yes. I am sure. And you, you are sad he go away?'

Charlotte nodded, still trying to take in the fact that Rohan had declared he loved her. It could not be true. He loved Merelda. There had to be some misunderstanding.

By the time Isabel left, hopping on to her motorcycle and burbling her way up the mountain road, Charlotte felt thoroughly confused. Rohan must have said something to Alberto but it couldn't have concerned her. Perhaps Rohan had taken Merelda there also. Perhaps it was Merelda Alberto was thinking of. Perhaps it was Isabel who was wrong.

Again her night was spent tossing and turning, her mind in complete turmoil. *Rohan loved her*! It was not possible. *Rohan loved her*! No, he didn't, he loved Merelda. *Rohan loved her*! No, no, Rohan had used her; all he had wanted was to take his revenge.

Her next visitor was Teresa, driving a battered Jeep and unloading two huge boxes of supplies. Charlotte had to smile when she saw the woman. Far from being the ravishing beauty she had suspected, Teresa must have been all of about seventy, and she spoke not a word of English. Nevertheless, they managed through mime to establish that Charlotte was coping well and there was nothing else she needed.

Four days went by, four long, empty days—days filled with sadness, anger, sorrow, and remorse; and soon it would be time for her to go home too. And the sad thing was that her holiday had done her no good at all. She still seemed to have a permanent headache, still felt tired all the time.

When Rohan walked into the villa the next afternoon she did not know whether to be pleased or not. One half of her was climbing sky-high because the man she loved and wanted to spend the rest of her life with was back; her other, more prosaic half felt resentful over the way he had treated her, the way he had played with her emotions and then left her high and dry, over the way he had chosen Merelda in preference to her.

She had been out sunbathing and was now sitting indoors, still in her bikini, thinking about Rohan, the radio on—which was the reason she had not heard his car—and it was an immense shock when he suddenly appeared.

All she could do was stare at him in surprise. Did it mean what she hoped it meant—or was the punishment to continue? She wanted to jump up and run into his arms but knew that would be a big mistake. There was nothing on his face to say that *he* was pleased to be back. Whatever his reason it was not because he loved her. Without a doubt Isabel had been mistaken.

'How are you, Charlotte?' He put down his case, threw his jacket, which he had been carrying, on top of it, and dropped into a chair. He looked totally exhausted, lines of strain on his face that had not been there before.

'I'm fine,' she answered.

'You don't look fine.' It was a gruff accusation. 'You look as though you haven't slept a wink since I left.'

She shrugged. 'I guess I was a bit scared on my own.'

'There was no need; you're quite safe here. Have you been eating properly? Did Teresa come?'

'Yes.'

'And Isabel?'

'Every day after work.'

'You haven't been too lonely?'

As if he cared! Lord, he was handsome. Her stomach muscles bunched and her whole body called out to him.

She wanted to be held in those strong, sinewy arms; she wanted to feel his body against hers; she wanted—everything.

'I've enjoyed my solitude,' she lied. 'How about you? Is everything sorted? No more problems?' Small talk, small talk; God, how she hated it.

He closed his eyes and dropped his head back. 'For the time being.'

'You're tired. Can I get you anything.'

'A double whisky would be nice.'

And so she poured his drink and put it on the table beside him but when she spoke softly he did not answer and she saw that he was asleep. Her heart went out to him and she gently touched the back of her finger to his cheek. He did not stir. She leaned over him and touched the same spot with her lips. It was probably the last time she would ever be able to do this. And then she sat back in her chair and looked at him.

His thick hair was awry, as though he had run his fingers through it several times on the journey, and the new lines that had appeared on his face were relaxed in sleep, almost gone. His chest lifted and fell, lifted and fell.

It looked as though she had been wrong and it *was* problems at work that had taken him away. He looked as though he had worked too hard and too long with too little sleep. Then the flight over here and the long drive afterwards. He ought to have gone straight to bed. But then she wouldn't have been able to study him like this. She liked looking at him; she liked the feeling it gave her; the trouble was she wanted to touch him again. The craving was so great that she began to get to her feet when suddenly he opened his eyes, so she sat back down again, her heart bumping violently.

He blinked and shook his head. 'I must have fallen asleep; I'm sorry.'

'Don't apologise,' she said. 'Why don't you drink your whisky and then go to bed for an hour or two?'

'Because we need to talk.'

Charlotte frowned. About what? 'Surely it can wait?'

'No, it can't,' he declared firmly; 'it's why I came back. I owe you an apology, Charlotte.'

'You do?' she asked in surprise. 'What for?' Playing games? Hurting her? Had he suddenly had an attack of conscience?

'For doubting you.'

Her eyes widened. This wasn't quite what she had expected.

'I caused you a great deal of unnecessary pain.'

'Unnecessary?' she asked sharply.

He heaved a sigh and sat forward in his chair, his hands linked between his knees. 'I saw Barry Fernhough. I found out the true reason you dumped him.'

Charlotte's eyes flashed as she all at once realised what he was getting at. 'Are you saying that you believe his word and yet you wouldn't believe mine?'

'I'm sorry,' he said quietly.

'Being sorry isn't good enough,' she snapped. Lord, did he really expect her to accept his apology after all the pain he had put her through?

'If you'd only told me the whole truth,' he groaned. 'I had no idea that he'd been two-timing you, or that it was his lover's husband who put him out of business.'

'I shouldn't have needed to tell you,' she cried; 'you should have taken my word. Have you any idea what it's like to be accused of something you're not guilty of?'

'I'm beginning to,' he said ruefully. 'I've really messed up your life, haven't I? Will you ever forgive me?'

Charlotte closed her eyes. It was good that at last he had accepted that she wasn't a gold-digger, but it made little difference now. It was his love she wanted more than anything else and that was the last thing on offer.

'Charlotte?'

She realised she had not answered his question. 'It really doesn't matter.' Her tone was flat and lifeless.

'To me it does,' he growled. 'I also bumped into a friend of Glen's. She's a lot like I imagined you to be.'

Charlotte looked at him questioningly.

'She used to go out with Glen, many years ago before he met you, and even after he got married she still made a nuisance of herself. It was Ginny he was referring to when he said he had been pestered for money and it was in danger of spoiling his marriage.' He shook his head slowly and sadly. 'I got it wrong all along the line, Charlotte.'

'So, now you know I'm not the gold-digger you thought,' she said with false gaiety. 'But you didn't have to come back here to tell me that. It would have waited.'

'I didn't want to wait,' he told her, sounding suddenly serious. 'It was far too important.'

'I don't see why,' she said.

'Because there's something else I have to tell you.' He got up and came to her, kneeling at her feet, taking her hands, and looking into her face. 'I love you, Charlotte.'

A few days ago, before Merelda, before he had told her it was all a game, she would have been ecstatic, but not now. She looked at him coldly. 'And I'm expected to believe that, am I? I'm expected to believe that your game of revenge is over? That you're sorry about it? Let's pretend it never happened; let's kiss and be friends.

Is that it? I don't happen to believe in one-sided love-affairs, Rohan.'

He groaned and the pain in his eyes was very real. 'Oh, Charlotte, that was never my intention.'

She looked at him scornfully. 'Don't play the innocent with me, Rohan Courtenay. It's perfectly clear what you were doing. You thought you'd try and get me to fall in love with you so that you could then ditch me and hurt me as you thought I'd hurt Glen.'

'Charlotte!' He looked scandalised.

'Are you denying it?' she asked coldly, her chin high, her eyes bright.

'Of course I'm denying it; even I wouldn't sink that low. Charlotte, my darling, how could I do that to a girl I love? My biggest fight has been with myself. The day you injured yourself in the forest, when you were so long coming, I nearly went out of my mind with worry.' He took a deep, ragged breath. 'I know you don't love me, and I can't blame you after the way I've treated you, but there is something there, isn't there? Perhaps you could learn to love me too in time?'

'Never!' she cried. 'Even if you haven't been taking revenge you're still a bastard, and an even bigger one for waiting until you got proof that I'm not a gold-digger before declaring your feelings. You're a louse and I hate you and I never want to see you again. Go back; go back home, go back to Merelda, go and leave me in peace.'

'Merelda means nothing to me, Charlotte,' he told her imploringly. 'You must believe that. It was all in *her* mind; it was what *she* wanted, not me; I played along with it to try and make you jealous but—hell, it didn't work; it only made matters worse.'

'OK, so you don't love Merelda,' she said ungraciously. 'There's still the fact that you needed proof.'

He looked pained. 'Charlotte, it's not like that.'

'Then what is it like?' she demanded. 'It sounds pretty cut and dried to me.'

'I wanted to tell you how I felt before I left. Couldn't you see that? Couldn't you tell? I really thought I was getting somewhere with you. If only Merelda hadn't turned up when she did. But then I thought what was the use when you didn't love me? I knew I couldn't stay here and keep silent. It wasn't work that took me back to England, my sweet Charlotte, and it wasn't Merelda either; it was you. My love was killing me; I couldn't stand it any longer.'

'But you went to see Barry,' she accused.

'No, no, no!' he exclaimed. 'We met accidentally through a mutual business friend. He was shocked that I could think such a thing of you. I have to admit I'm truly ashamed of myself, and completely repentant.'

Charlotte felt a spiral of hope begin to climb, feelings that had taken a fierce battering during the last few minutes starting to revive. She looked deep into Rohan's eyes and saw nothing but humility and love and she suddenly knew how much it had cost him to come back and say these words.

She smiled, faintly at first, and then it broke into a broad, unstoppable grin.

'Is something funny?' A puzzled frown creased his brow.

'Get up, Rohan, I don't want you at my feet.'

'I felt it was where I belonged,' he said humbly.

'Not now, not ever,' she told him, and her voice was strong and full of confidence. 'I have something to tell you too.'

He waited.

'Kiss me first,' she said.

Another faint frown, hesitation, suspicion, and then he pulled her hard against him and his mouth covered hers and the flow of hunger didn't want to be stemmed.

This was a real kiss, thought Charlotte; it was a kiss full of love and longing, the release of pent-up emotions, a declaration of love. And she had no hesitation about responding; she gave him her all, parting her lips, accepting his ever-deepening kiss, crying out, moving her body sensuously against his, feeling his arousal, revelling in it.

How long it was before he lifted his head she had no idea—time lost all meaning, pleasure was paramount. But eventually, reluctantly, he drew back and looked at her. 'Was that supposed to tell me something, Charlotte?'

She nodded and felt suddenly shy.

'Does it mean what I think it means?'

'Yes, Rohan,' she said huskily. 'It means I love you too; it means I'm so glad you love me; it means I'm so glad you came back; it means I never thought this moment would happen.'

She felt the waves of surprise ripple through him; she felt his pleasure, his warmth, his happiness.

'Charlotte, my darling, my dear, sweet girl, I never dreamt—I hoped but never thought it possible. Is it true?'

She nodded.

'I want you to marry me,' he declared joyfully. 'I want you to be my wife; I want you to be mine.'

'I want to be yours too,' she said shyly.

He kissed her again and then they sat down and held each other close. 'All these years I've loved you,' he said, 'right from the very first moment I met you. I truly meant it when I said that if I'd met you first Glen wouldn't have stood a chance. God, how I envied him.'

'I think I loved you as well,' she said.

'And I stupidly ruined everything by accusing you of deeds I should have known you were not capable of committing. Will you ever truly be able to forgive me?'

'I already have.'

'You're too good for me,' he groaned.

'I wonder what Douglas will say?'

Rohan's lips twisted wryly. 'I've already told him how I feel. He's glad I've come to my senses at last. And he was pretty confident that you felt the same way. He's looking forward to welcoming you into the family for the second time.'

'And who's going to run Courtenay Textiles? Will we live in London?'

'I'm afraid we'll have to, my sweetheart, but I intend to buy a house on the Thames so it won't be too bad. And my father's business—well, we both thought it would be a good idea to sell out completely, perhaps to Miguel Correia. And my father's going to come and live with us—well, not exactly with us but we'll find him somewhere close by.'

It looked as though father and son had done a lot of hard talking while she was here and Rohan was in England, while she was unhappy and he was making plans. Her smile felt as though it was splitting her face in two. 'I've never been happier, Rohan.'

'Not even when you married Glen?'

'I thought I was,' she confessed, serious for a moment, 'but I actually don't think I ever loved him as a man should truly be loved; more as a friend, I think.'

'But you made him happy,' he told her, 'and for that I will always be grateful.'

'I want to make you happy now,' she said softly.

'And you will, just by being my wife. Oh, Charlotte.' He gathered her to him and kissed her again and again. 'This is for life, isn't it?'

She nodded.

'I won't fail you,' he promised.

'I know.' And this time her submission was complete.

LEGACY of LOVE

An exciting range of 4 historical romances from mediaeval settings to the turn of the 20th Century.

Each month features 1 much loved Regency romance along with an increasing variety of romance with historical backgrounds such as the French Revolution and the Californian Gold Rush.

Price: £2.50

MILLS & BOON

Available from WH Smith, John Menzies, Volume One, Forbuoys, Martins, Woolworths, Tesco, Asda, Safeway and other paperback stockists.

Barbara DELINSKY

A COLLECTION

New York Times bestselling author Barbara Delinsky has created three wonderful love stories featuring the charming and irrepressible matchmaker, Victoria Lesser. Worldwide are proud to bring back these delightful romances – together for the first time, they are published in one beautiful volume this September.

**THE REAL THING
TWELVE ACROSS
A SINGLE ROSE**

Available from September   Priced £4.99

WORLDWIDE

Available from WH Smith, John Menzies, Volume One, Forbuoys, Martins, Woolworths, Tesco, Asda, Safeway and other paperback stockists.

NORA ROBERTS

A COLLECTION

From the best-selling author of *Hot Ice* and *Sweet Revenge* comes a dazzling collection of three early novels, beautifully presented in one absorbing volume.

THE LAST HONEST WOMAN
DANCE TO THE PIPER
SKIN DEEP

Three impulsive sisters, three intimate encounters, three sensuous and unforgettable love stories.

AVAILABLE NOW **PRICE £4.99**

WORLDWIDE

Available from WH Smith, John Menzies, Volume One, Forbuoys, Martins, Woolworths, Tesco, Asda, Safeway and other paperback stockists.

FOR BETTER FOR WORSE

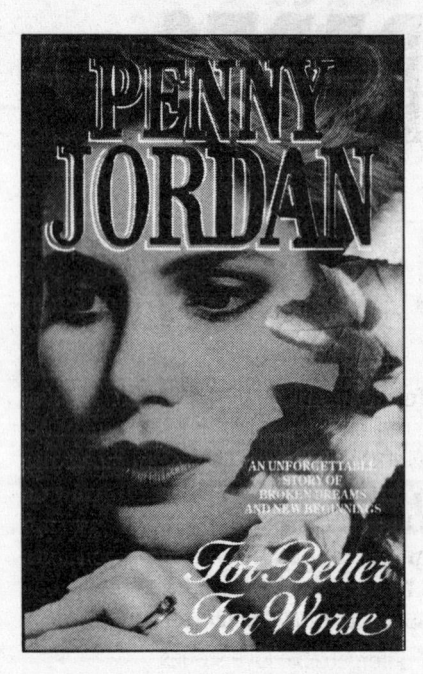

They would each face life's bittersweet choices in their search for love...

Penny Jordan has created a masterpiece of raw emotion, with this dramatic novel which takes a fascinating and, at times, painfully telling look at three couples' hopes, dreams and desires.

A story of obsessions...
A story of choices...
A story of love.

AVAILABLE NOW

PRICED: £4.99

WORLDWIDE

Available from WH Smith, John Menzies, Volume One, Forbuoys, Martins, Woolworths, Tesco, Asda, Safeway and other paperback stockists.